# Help Me Hannah

# Barbara Pressman

ISBN Number: 979-8-4685507-3-1

# Dedication

To all who came before and all who came after:

*My Grandparents*—Simon and Tessie & Benjamin and Mollie. You gave me the best examples of the immigrant experience.

*My Parents*—Alvin and Hannah. Your stories and reflections of your childhood inspired me to look deeper.

*My Brother and Sister*—Ken and Diana, who shared my childhood with me, and especially my late sister Laura who was the real writer in the family.

*My two Sons and their Spouses* – Matt and Shiri & Mike and Adam. You are the heart of this family.

*My Grandchildren*—Lily and Maya. You keep me young and fill my life with joy.

Most of all, my strong, intelligent and loving husband, **Roger**. Thank you for being in my life for over 50 wonderful years.

# Acknowledgements

Writing this book has been a team effort. I want to thank my husband, Roger, for his insightful edits and suggestions. He also helped me with the cover design, the format, and the final upload to Amazon—no small task! His technical expertise was invaluable. But most of all, his encouragement gave me the confidence to write this novel.

I also want to thank my early readers—Judith Beiner, Susan Shaber, Aggie Winthrop, Carol Guido, and Andrea Bader. Their comments and suggestions helped me to shape the story, the characters and the outcome.

# Introduction

My father, Al Laster, was larger than life in my eyes. He was a dentist, but it was always his dream to be a professional writer. Throughout his life, he wrote beautiful, award-winning poetry, along with articles for local newspapers and even a piece published in the *New York Times*. But for me, his most important body of work was an extensive family history, *Echoes from the Attic*. Spiral-bound and printed on a 1980s-era dot matrix printer, my father's book was written for his children—to remind us all of the family members who came before us.

During the pandemic of 2020, I once again took out his spiral bound book and lost myself in the detailed memoir. It contains stories and photos of *the old country*, immigrants arriving at Ellis Island from Hungary, his aunts and uncles, and neighbors. My mother, Hannah, wrote a chapter about her Lithuanian family. In her opinion, they were a bit more "cultured" than the coarse Hungarians on my father's side, but that was a matter of continuing debate. Each of my parents described in vivid detail what life was like growing up during the depression.

As a child, I was lucky enough to be surrounded by this loving cast of characters. I remember lying in bed with my grandmother while she reminisced about her life back in Hungary. With a far-away gaze, she would revisit the old country, her thick accent adding texture to her words.

"My family owned a huge farm and we lived in a big house with many servants. We had a storage room, with barrels of pickles and sauerkraut, potatoes, and beets. We even had beer kegs to sell at the tavern.

"And look at me now," she would moan, despair in her voice.

*Echoes from the Attic* brought it all back. I recalled relatives who would visit on Saturdays, my Dad's day off, to get their teeth fixed. This free service was provided in my Dad's dental office conveniently attached to our house.

Uncle Freddy with black kinky hair, thick Hungarian accent and a big space between his teeth, and a big loud laugh that would fill the room. His wife, Aunt Bella, who my grandmother called a hussy, with her *Za Za Gabor* accent and large gold hoop earrings, a cigarette dangling from her mouth as she spoke. We kids were sure that she was a gypsy. And there was quiet cousin Richard with tattooed numbers on his arm. And Uncle Carl, the barber, with a lift in his shoe.

That cast of characters, along with many others, was my family. I wanted to bring them back to life.

And that is how **Help Me Hannah** was born.

# Part 1: New York City–1933

## Transition to Widowhood

Quiet … there it is again. I can't seem to escape the dreaded quiet. How I long for the noise of daily conversation. I'm trying to relax and read *The Forward,* but I can't concentrate. Loneliness washes over me like a dark cloud.

It was anything but quiet during the *shiva,*[1] that week of mourning when my parents, my in-laws, my brother, and oh-so-many friends came to visit, schmooze, and pay their respects. That was last week.

This week is different. My parents are back home, in Bridgeport. Friends have said goodbye, done their part. They promise to help if I ever need them. They'll keep in touch, they say. But I know I'll be on my own. In the end, we're always on our own. I'm alone with my thoughts, my fears, my memories. All that's left of that comforting time of *shiva* is one last single, lonely piece of mandel bread. I decide to make some tea to go with that last bit of sweetness, and sit at my kitchen table, and try again to read *The Forward* in Yiddish. Yes, I'm indulging myself. And I'm not ashamed.

---

[1] A glossary of Yiddish words and expressions is presented at the end of this book.

Let me introduce myself.

My name is Hannah Altman. Up until 2 weeks ago, I was a happily married mother of two. I felt secure and content, mostly. Of course, I had my worries, what wife and mother doesn't?

But now, in the quiet, I feel like I'm lost in a maze of uncertainty and sadness.

It was jolting at first, that horrible day. My husband Abe, handsome and charming, only 46-years old, was recovering from gallbladder surgery. He was lying under the oxygen tent when my daughter, Frances, found him, no longer breathing. The hospital staff told me he died of post-operative pneumonia. I learned later that he also had cirrhosis of the liver. Abe had always loved to "have a drink with the boys," but he kept that kind of drinking a secret from me. I remember having a sinking feeling when he'd come home, wobbly and slightly disoriented, but I'd push the thought out of my head. Everything else about my husband was great, why dwell on the negative? "None of us is perfect," I would say to myself.

I remember so clearly the moment I realized how serious his drinking was. One evening, while Franny was walking home from a friend's apartment, she found her father sitting on the curb, leaning over himself. It killed me to know that Frances had to see him this way. "Mom, come out here. I can't get Daddy up off the curb. He won't move." The familiar sweet smell of alcohol on his breath was a jolt to my senses. Together we got him inside and into bed. I made light of it. I could see the look of horror and shame on Frances' face.

Thank goodness my son Solly never saw the dark side of his father. He was always warm and affectionate with the children. I'm quite sure that my Franny will remember him the way he was during his sober moments, full of laughter and life. I promised myself that I'd make sure of that.

I need to give myself a pep talk. I'm strong, intelligent, and resilient. "Yes, keep telling yourself that, Hannah." The truth is, I'm a widow - so young they all tell me. I need to find my strength, my skills, my abilities. "No rush," I tell myself. God will provide. He'll send me a sign. He always does.

I have always felt that God has a way of making things right for me. He did that on the night it all began, way back when I first met Abe at the Harlem Zionist Organization. It was a hot August night, 1920. I saw a pleasant looking young man sitting with some friends across the room. He caught my eye and winked. I gave him a smile of encouragement, and it seemed to work. After the meeting he introduced himself. "I saw you playing the mandolin," he said. "I admire anyone who has a talent for music."

"For me it's just a hobby," I told him. "But I love to play songs and have friends sing along.

Abe loved to hear me sing his favorite Russian Jewish folk song, *Tumbalalaika*. After we had Frances and Solly, we would all sing together in the evenings. Those are happy memories for me, and no one can take them away. Even though Abe is gone, the haunting song plays in my head.

*Tumbala Tumbala Tumbalalaika*...the words and melody of this Russian folk song lull me into a light sleep. My eyes close, my breath becomes steady, and I find solace in sleep. "I'll start planning for my future tomorrow," I think as I doze off.

*Tumbala, Tumbala, Tumbalalaika*

*Tumbala, Tumbala, Tumbalalaika*

*Tumbalalaika, Shpil balalaika*

*Tumbalalaika Frelekh zol zayn*

# Tessie's Visit

The sun rises, and I wake up, reaching for Abe. *Will I ever break this habit?* I think to myself.

Today there is no need to rush out of bed. It's Saturday. The kids are off from school, and I know that Tessie, my loyal best friend, will come for a visit today.

Let me tell you about Tessie. We have been friends since childhood. When we came to New York, I was eight and Tessie was nine. We played together on the street outside of our apartment building. We were both pretty good at jumping rope, especially Double Dutch. When we got tired of that, we'd play jacks or roller skate. Sometimes we'd make our own paper dolls out of newspaper.

Other friends would sometimes join us, but Tessie and I were always loyal to one another. I remember the time that little Sammy Raskin tried to steal my shiny new cat's eye marble. Tessie found out and grabbed it from his hand and smacked him on the head. He ran home crying. Yes, Tessie was fearless, a little *bonditt*.

Our lives have taken us in different directions. Now, Tessie and her husband Simon own a brownstone in Hoboken that Simon converted into a boarding house. Simon worked hard on the renovation. He's one of those people who can build and fix anything. If you look at his hands, you can see his strength. We like to tease him that his hands look like the paws.

I live across the river in an apartment in Washington Heights. Distance hasn't hurt our friendship. Even though our lives have gone in different directions, we've remained close. We both have children now. Motherhood is a common bond for us these days.

Tessie visits often, and now that Abe is gone, she promises to visit me every Saturday. It's a pretty big trip for Tessie—trolley, then ferry, then subway. But she does it, and I'm grateful. Tessie has a lot on her plate. She likes to confide in me, and because I'm a good listener, I actually enjoy her stories. They're always dramatic, and she's usually the cause of that drama. But, of course, she'll never admit to it.

"Let me wake the children," I say to myself. I walk into their shared bedroom. They're still asleep, thankfully. I look into those shiny, innocent faces, still immersed in dreams. The room has a slightly musty odor, combined with the sweet smell of sleeping children.

My thoughts quickly go dark. To lose a parent at such a young age? They'll be forced to become independent, and so will I ... I'll have to work. I can't depend on Abe for support anymore. Up until now, I've probably spoiled my kids. Spoiled them because I wanted to.

Because I'm a *greenhorn,* I'm often self-conscious of my dress, my speech patterns, my mannerisms. But my children? My children are true Americans, born in New York City, where the streets are "paved with gold," or so we were told. My father brought us over from Kovna, Lithuania when I was just eight years old. He loves to tell the story about sneaking our beautiful brass samovar on the boat. He wrapped it in a blanket, and my mother carried it, as if it was a baby. It's proudly displayed in my apartment now.

Now, people tell me that I speak English very well, even without an accent. I'm very proud of that. And I want my children to feel that way too. The old country is a thing of the past. Yes, let them be spoiled American kids. I *want* them to be spoiled American kids.

"Wake up sleepy head" I say to Solly, my little one. "Good Morning MMMMother," he says to me, with a big hug. Solly is ten and struggles with a stutter. I try to pretend not to notice. With his bright blue eyes and curly brown hair - his looks are dazzling to me. "Let's wake your sister up," I say lovingly.

"Mom, I heard you. Please let me sleep," Frances grumbles. Franny is my sensitive, serious child. She also has beautiful eyes—light hazel, with some green in them. Her face is round and symmetric. She has very straight brown hair, with bangs straight across her forehead. When she was little, I hoped that she would have curls, like Shirley Temple. But it turns out, with her straight brown hair, her style is more like Buster Brown.

My Franny is very smart, skipping two grades in school already. Her teachers tell me she has great promise. When I watch the way she interacts with Solly, I know she would be a fine teacher. Their favorite game is playing school. I tend to count on my reliable, steady girl to be my helper in life. So far, she's never let me down. She's fourteen years old already.

While they get dressed, I walk into the kitchen to make breakfast. As soon as I enter my favorite room my mood brightens. The stove sits in the center of the rear wall, the place where all the important work gets done. But the kitchen table is the centerpiece of the room—a family gathering place where all kinds of conversation and gossip flow. The children do their homework there, while I supervise from afar. The white eyelet cafe curtains add a special touch, especially in the spring when the window is open to let in a gentle breeze. Everything about my kitchen whispers "stay awhile."

I slice a few pieces of challah from last night's Shabbos dinner, and put butter and strawberry jam on each slice. I make coffee for myself, and a special drink for my kids. I call it a "guggle muggle." Abe invented that name. It's a tiny amount of coffee, mixed with lots of warm milk and sugar. The children feel like they are drinking a grownup drink. And I feel good that they're drinking lots of milk and getting a little wake up "kick" from the caffeine. What can it hurt?

We eat breakfast together. We all try *not* to acknowledge the empty chair at the head of the table. Bright and cheery conversation is just too difficult. We eat in silence. After breakfast I send the children out to play on the street. "Be careful out there," I tell them. Frances takes out her book to sit on the stoop and read. Maybe one of her friends will come by and ask her to play Jacks. Solly takes his *Spauldeen* ball. I know he'll look for a stick ball game somewhere. I hope he's not too shy to find one. His stuttering holds him back sometimes. As I clear the table, I decide to bake a new batch of mandel bread for my afternoon visit with Tessie. Baking is therapy for me. The feel of the dough, the warmth of the oven, brings my home to life. And oh...how Abe appreciated my baking.

Just as the doorbell rings, I finish putting a few slices of warm mandel bread on one of my fancy plates, with a few walnuts and red grapes. "Nice touch," I say to myself.

Tessie Lester walks in. Her strong perfume precedes her. I don't have the heart to tell my friend that she uses way too much. The essence of *Evening in Paris* fills the house and sadly, overpowers my baking smells. Tessie is a strong woman, very short and stocky. Abe used to say "She's built like an army tank." I would chastise him, but I'd giggle, anyway. Tessie's Hungarian accent and curly black hair make it hard for her to hide that she's a "greener." She sounds a little bit like the glamorous Gabor sisters, but that's where the resemblance ends. Being a greenhorn is something we all want to avoid. That's why we try to speak English without an accent. I avoid Yiddish expressions as much as I can. Not my Tessie. She really doesn't care the way I do. Or maybe she just can't help it. Nonetheless that's Tessie.

"So, *nu* Hannah? How are you?" Tessie gives me a big hug to show me that she's aware of my sadness today. "I know this can't be easy for you, my friend."

"I'm trying to get used to the fact that I'm alone now," I say, trying not to break down. Tessie's empathy makes me vulnerable. I can feel myself tearing up.

"I never realized how much I depended on Abe all these years. I took it all for granted," I tell Tessie, shaking my head. If there's anyone I can open up to, it's Tessie. "Some days I can't even get out of bed."

Tessie gives me another hug and asks, "How will you pay your rent, put food on the table?"

Leave it to Tessie to be blunt and shake me into reality again. That's why I can tell her anything. I trust her to always tell me the truth.

"Abe sold insurance, so of course I have some money from insurance payments. He was responsible that way. But it certainly won't be enough for the three of us long term. I do have a possible solution. There's a job opportunity that has come up, and I'm hoping it will work out," I say with some trepidation in my voice.

"Really? So soon?" Tessie responds. "Are you sure you'll be able to work? Who will watch Frances and Solly?"

Just as the words come out of her mouth, the children come in from playing outside. "Mrs. Lester. Mrs. Lester." With that, Tessie gives each child a round peppermint candy from her pocketbook, which she snaps open and snaps shut. My kids love that sound. They think that purse must hold all kinds of magical things. They thank her, and then she adds a special gift. "Here *mein kinder*, a little *gelt* for you. "She dramatically takes out a nickel for each child, one for each hand, and tells them to go buy something special for themselves. Solly is grinning from ear to ear, and even Frances breaks down and smiles.

When the children leave, I tell Tessie about my job offer. My Uncle Ben Bader, "the doctor," as my whole family proudly calls him, has an office one block away from my apartment, on St. Nicholas Avenue in Washington Heights. We are so proud of him for getting his graduate degree from Fordham Medical School. Uncle Ben tells me that he will soon need a receptionist/medical assistant to replace Aunt Rose, his wife, who is pregnant. Uncle Ben and Aunt Rose are the pride of our family, both very well educated. They bring such prestige to us. The entire family is excited for them as we await the birth of their new baby.

Aunt Rose has worked alongside her husband since he started his practice. A traditional woman who will soon become a stay-at-home mother, she wears her hair in two long braids, which she winds around her head, making a neat little *crown*. And then there are the pearls, which give her an extra measure of sophistication. Rose can be a little bossy and intimidating at times, but I admire her.

"And that's where I come in," I say to Tessie. "The timing is perfect for me. I'll need an income. They'll need help in the office. But I have so many questions in my mind, Tessie. Will I have the skills, the personality, the *chutzpah* to run a medical practice? Will Frances and little Solly manage at home without me?"

Tessie rolls her eyes and gives me a "look." I know that look. "Of course, you can handle it Hannah. You've managed a household for 15 years now. What makes you think you can't take on more responsibility? And besides, Abe wasn't around all that much to help you when he was alive." Her head tilts to the side a little. Those words sink like a stone in my heart.

So, I change the subject. "How have you been Tessie? How are little Alvin and Alice? Is Alice still dating that boy?" Tessie's expression changes.

"The kids are okay, Hannah. But Simon has lost his job again. Thank goodness I have the boarding house to keep us afloat. Simon always has the same excuse. He tells me his boss is an anti-Semite. That excuse is getting old, Hannah." According to Simon, everyone's an anti-Semite. I've heard this story too many times already.

Tessie continues. "And my beautiful Alice? She's still dating that boy Joe. She can do better. Alvin, my dreamer, is busy writing little poems and playing jokes on the family. Now he's learning magic tricks, a regular Harry Houdini. In school, his teacher tells me he daydreams all day long, and he may have to stay back a year. But I know how smart he is. He's just so small for his age. Maybe not so interested in school. That teacher doesn't know what she's talking about. She's *meshuggeh*. I think she's in love with my Alvin and wants to keep him in her third-grade class forever." There she goes again, my Tessie, always with drama in her life. Imagined or real, it's always drama.

"These are hard times for all of us Tessie. Jobs are hard to come by. Simon tries his best." In my heart though, I am concerned. Simon has a way of making enemies at work. He's an excellent mechanic. He has skills, great with his hands. But, what a temper. Doesn't he realize we're in a depression right now? Jobs are scarce. A man can't afford to lose his temper on the job. Not these days, I think to myself.

Just a few crumbs remain on the plate as we finish our little *nosh* and our conversation. I walk her out to the front stoop. Solly is hitting the ball against the step, all by himself. His smile is gone. I know he's thinking about his dad. My motherly instincts kick in. "Solly, say goodbye to Mrs. Lester." He gives a perfunctory wave and goes back to his *Spauldeen* ball. Then I have an idea.

"Tessie, why don't you bring Alvin here one day to play with Solly. My son will be a perfect audience for his magic tricks."

As I watch Tessie walk away, her squat frame shrinking as she moves further down the block, I feel the loneliness creep up on me. Tessie's visit was a nice distraction, but now I must face being alone once again. "Get used to it, Hannah," I say to myself.

I return to my kitchen and open up *The Forward* again. I didn't get very far last night. My favorite section is *A Bintel Brief*— the advice column. Each week I love to read the stories of new immigrants arriving in NYC with hardly a dime in their pockets. They still possess those old European customs, which don't really work here. They are surprised to see that the streets are *not* paved with gold. Their travails make mine look pretty minor. Do I sound a little smug? Problems are problems, big or small. They're always big if they're your own. But reading the problems in *A Bintel Brief* gives me insight and courage. Sometimes I try to put myself in the editor's shoes. What advice would I give? Usually, the editor and I are pretty close in our thinking.

# Recipe for Mandel Bread

In my life the best conversations and the best advice, happen around the kitchen table with a cup of tea and mandel bread. Since I talk about it constantly, here's my favorite mandel bread recipe.

**1 stick of butter**
**3 eggs**
**1 t Vanilla extract**
**¼ cup Vegetable oil**
**3 cups flour**
**1 t baking powder**
**¾ chopped walnuts, chopped almonds, or pecans**

Melt butter
Beat 3 eggs with 1 cup sugar
Add 1 t vanilla
Add ¼ cup oil and melted butter
Add 3 heaping cups flour and 1t baking powder
Add chopped nuts
Form into 3 long strips

Bake at 375 degrees for 25 minutes or until firm. Then let cool. Slice on angle. Put slices back on cookie sheet. Turn oven up to 425 degrees. Bake 5 minutes, then turn and bake another 5 minutes, until golden brown.

# A Job Interview

As I get dressed for my interview at Uncle Ben's office this Tuesday morning, I think about my previous work experience. What do I have to offer for this job? When I was a child in school, I learned to read and write and do embroidery. My classroom was always crowded, with straight rows of wooden desks. Our teachers were very strict so we learned to behave through fear. But I always loved reciting the Pledge Alliance to the Flag. I felt proud to be an American. And I always won the spelling bee for my grade.

Money was tight, so one summer my parents sent me out to work when I was only twelve years old, working in a hat factory nearby. Although they weren't supposed to, they hired children. Because of the famous Triangle Shirtwaist Factory Fire, there were rules in place for safety, and of course child labor was forbidden. That fire was a tragedy that no one is New York will ever forget because 146 workers died due to horrible working conditions. After that, unions became more powerful, and better laws were set in place. But not everyone followed those rules.

One morning, during my first week, an inspector came into the factory to check on working conditions. My supervisor quickly hid me in a large carton until he left. I stayed perfectly still for over an hour. It felt like a lifetime. And I didn't get caught. When I was finally let out, I felt proud that I had kept the secret.

Working in the factory was hard—long hours and horrible working conditions. I started off sweeping the floor. Later, I helped the sewing machine operators, doing odd jobs, easy ones, like cutting threads. I watched the others, and learned a few things. The best part was that I brought money home for the family.

Sewing and millinery are just hobbies for me now. I enjoy making clothes for Frances and myself. I proudly wear the hats that I design, especially during high holiday services at synagogue. My hats are adorned with ostrich feathers and beading. But let's face it, the hat making experience will not really be helpful in Uncle Ben's doctor's office.

I know Aunt Rose asked me to be her replacement for a reason. Perhaps this job offer is charity. Oh…. I hate the idea of being a charity case. Dr. Ben Bader and his wife are known as kind people. I know they want to help.

So…..I put on a crisp white blouse and a navy blue wool skirt. My hair is curled in a classic pageboy style, with a pompadour curl on top. My hair shines because I brushed it one hundred strokes last night before bed. I glance in the mirror before leaving. "Not bad," I say, giving myself a little smile and a boost. "Not too bad."

I march out the door and walk around the corner to Uncle Ben's office. I knock on the door and Aunt Rose lets me in. She gives me a hug. The tears begin to flow. For some reason, when anyone shows me kindness and sympathy, my eyes well up with tears. I pull myself together. "Good morning, Aunt Rose. Thank you for giving me the opportunity to interview for this job."

"Nonsense Hannah. I need to find a replacement for myself. My belly is growing and soon it will be embarrassing to work here. You know how people can be. A pregnant woman does not belong in the workplace. It doesn't look nice."

Aunt Rose is being kind to me today. But I know what she's thinking. Poor Hannah. A widow at such a young age. How will she support herself, Frances, and little Solly? I fight the urge to cry once again. Swallowing hard, I try to sound professional. "What will my responsibilities be?"

"You will welcome the patients, bring them to the examining room. You'll take a short medical history, take their height and weight on the scale. After the visit, you'll take payments. You will keep the appointment book. Sometimes your Uncle Ben gets carried away and takes too long with his patients. We have a secret system to remind him that the next patient is waiting. You will give 3 knocks on the door to remind him." She goes on to tell me that I will be her "shadow" for the first week. Once I am able to handle the job alone, Aunt Rose will hand over the responsibility to me. This is the proposal.

"I would like to give this a try, Aunt Rose. But you must promise me that if I don't do a good job, you'll tell me. I don't want to be a burden." In my mind, I know my English is pretty good. My penmanship is excellent. But my confidence is a little shaky. Those sewing skills are not going to be much help in a doctor's office.

Aunt Rose says, "Are you ready to start tomorrow?" This is all happening very fast. I had better say yes. No point in delaying. Too much time to think could cause me to be even more nervous.

"Yes, Aunt Rose. I would like to start tomorrow."

I plan on speaking with Frances and Solly about it tonight. They are good children. Franny is like a little mother already. That was Abe's nickname for her - *Little Mother*. Frances loved the sound of it. It made her smile and blush. Now Frances, I think to myself, let's see if you can live up to your reputation.

# Stuttering

It's 3:00 pm and the children run into the apartment, happy that another day at school is over. Frances and Solly always run. Why do children do that? They never seem to walk unless they're forced to.

I have their milk and cookies ready for them.

"So, tell me, how was school today?" I ask.

Solly answers first, stuttering more than usual. "We're practicing our times tables. Mrs. Stevens wants us to mmmmmemorize them and recite them in fffffront of the class." Frances leans over and gently touches Solly's arm. "Don't worry Solly. I'll help you. We can practice together. Then when you get up to recite in class, you'll be prepared." Yes, I think to myself. *Little Mother.* Now I feel a bit more secure leaving them alone after school.

As they eat their after-school snack, I rehearse how I'm going to tell them about my new job. I'll talk about how wonderful it will be to work in a doctor's office and how we're all proud of Uncle Ben. I wait a beat and then begin.

"It's so wonderful to have a doctor in our family, such educated people. We should be very proud," I say.

The children give me a curious look. My statement came out of the blue, after all.

"And there is something else you should know. Your Uncle Ben, has offered me a job working in his doctor's office. I will take the place of Aunt Rose. You remember I told you that your aunt is going to have a baby?" The children nod, but now there is a look of concern on their faces. "What's wrong?" I ask.

Frances says, "Does that mean we'll be alone after school? Will I be taking care of Solly?"

I decide to use my negotiating skills here. Flattery usually works.

"Remember how your father used to call you Little Mother? Here's your chance to prove him right. Think of how proud of you he would be right now."

With that, Frances gets up and says to her brother, "Solly, let's start practicing those multiplication tables."

A good start, I decide. The rest will come in time. After supper, we'll talk about tying a key on a chain around her neck, and what to do until I arrive home on school days.

The next morning, after the children are safely off to school, I walk over to the office, wearing the white uniform that Rose has lent me. Luckily it fits. I begin my training slowly, observing Aunt Rose's words and motions. She greets each patient, takes their weight and height. She guides them into the examining room and takes a brief history, then asks why they have come in. She then states, "Dr. Bader will be with you shortly."

Between patients, she sits at her desk. "I think I can do this," I say to myself, but I don't dare say it out loud at the risk of sounding overly confident. All day long I watch and listen. Rose says, "Our last patient is an easy one. Her name is Sylvia Perlman. She's a *regular*. Dare I say a hypochondriac? Why don't you take Mrs. Perlman yourself Hannah? I'll be in the room with you. We'll work together. I think you're ready to give it a try."

I greet Mrs. Perlman, take her height and weight and guide her into the examining room. I ask her the basic questions for medical history, and I ask why she has come in today. I feel as if my voice is a little shaky. "Well, can't you see why I'm here? Look at the redness around my eye? You're not very observant. Who is this woman Rose?"

"I'll take over from here dear," Rose says, giving me a "look." I leave and go to sit at the desk. When Aunt Rose comes out of the room she gently reprimands me. We discuss the importance of knowing the patients and displaying confidence. She suggests that I was unsure of myself and that made Mrs. Perlman uneasy. "Perhaps I gave you too much responsibility too soon," she says. I try not to get defensive. This wasn't my fault. Mrs. Perlman *is* difficult.

"Always remember to display confidence, even when you are not feeling it. It puts the patients at ease. That's a big part of the job. I need you to work on that before you take over.

It's very important for me to know that the office will run smoothly without me." Aunt Rose is clearly irritated, which is troubling, of course.

"Here is another little tip, Hannah. When you feel shy, it's easy to make conversation with strangers. I have always found that people love to talk about themselves. All you need to do is ask a few questions to get them started. Then, look interested. The rest will take care of itself," Aunt Rose smiles.

Uncle Ben asks me how my first day went as we lock up the office. He has always been so good to me, and all of the family. I wonder if Rose might be jealous of that closeness. I tell him it went quite well, deciding not to mention the Mrs. Perlman incident. I tell him that I still have a lot to learn. "Of course, you do, Hannah. My dear wife will show you the ropes. You'll be an expert by the end of the week, I predict," Ben laughs.

When I get home the children are waiting and hungry. I had nearly forgotten about fixing dinner. Just as I trained today for my job, I must train my Franny for her job. More than just a baby sitter. I'd like her to get dinner ready too. She needs to learn how to get things started. I think about making my chicken fricassee on Friday, and she will be my helper. Each weekend, I decide, she will assist me in preparing supper. After a while, she'll have the basics under her belt.

I decide to fry up some salmon patties and noodles for dinner. While working in the kitchen, I hear Solly practicing the times tables with Frances. He seems to have forgotten his stutter. Oh, I hope this is a pattern will be repeated when he has to recite in school. But as soon as he starts talking, the stutter returns. Even a little progress is welcomed.

Melancholy sinks in now. The children staying home alone, Solly's speech problem, insecurity about the job all weigh heavily. When Abe was alive, if I felt weak or uncertain, he was always there to calm me down and give me a boost. I know if he were still with me he would grab me in his arms for the hug. Oh, he was such a great hugger. "Everything will be fine Hannah," he'd say with a laugh. And I guess I was dumb enough to believe him.

When everyone is in bed, I take out today's *Forward*, which I picked up at the newsstand on the way home. I settle into my usual routine of reading *A Bintel Brief*.[2] Today's letter is interesting to me. I enjoy getting lost in other people's problems.

*Dear Editor,*

*I hope you can help me with a problem. I don't speak Yiddish, so I have asked a friend to write this letter for me.*

*I am twenty-five years old, married to a kind man, a cab driver who earns very little. I never dreamed of riches and luxury. Our home is*

---

2  The letter that follows has been loosely adapted from a letter in *The Jewish Daily Forward* circa 1935.

*comfortable and clean. We have a two-year old daughter who is our whole life.*

*My husband doesn't drink or gamble. We love each other and lead a happy life. But ... I am not Jewish. My mother-in-law does not approve of me because of that.*

*She comes to visit every day for the sake of the grandchild, whom she loves dearly. She ignores me.*

*My husband loves me, but he also loves his mother. His love for his mother is very strange. My husband is tall, handsome, and well built. He turns into a child when he is with her. They kiss and hug. My mother-in-law comments that he looks bad when he really looks fine. She insinuates that I don't take care of him. I have ruined her son. If not for me, he would have married a wealthy Jewish girl. I occasionally answer back with a sharp word. Then she complains to my husband and there's havoc in the house.*

*I complain to my own mother about this. She tells me I must treat my mother-in-law with respect. I am a high school graduate and pretty nice looking. I get along well with the rest of my husband's family. I try to get along with my mother-in-law but she discourages it. I'm only afraid she may ruin our family life.*

*I beg you to suggest how I should deal with the situation*

*With great respect,*

*Deborah*

*Answer:*

    *The writer seems to be a very bright young lady. She understands the situation and is very patient. I advise you to be cordial to your mother in-law. Don't try to win her over. She will come around in time, especially because of the grandchild. The writer's own mother gave her good advice. She is a wise woman, just like her daughter.*

# A New Patient

As I leave for work on this crisp clear morning, I feel a burst of energy and a sense of pride as well. I've been working at Uncle Ben's office for three months and now I'm a true receptionist. Aunt Rose still hovers over me sometimes, which makes me nervous, but I can sense that she is more secure with the way I've been handling my duties.

Her pregnancy has progressed normally, and her due date is only one month away. She has that pregnant walk now, legs wide apart. The job is mine, with Rose dropping by to "check-up" on occasion. With a critical eye, she rearranges the pencils on the desk, wipes off the counter in the examining room. I think she wants to keep me off balance, just a little bit. It's hard for her to let go.

Aunt Rose is worried about her "late in life" baby, but they had to wait until Uncle Ben paid off his medical school loans and absorbed the expense of setting up his office. And then conceiving became a challenge, perhaps because they were both over 30.

I hope Rose won't be too high-strung for motherhood. Sometimes when women are older, they lack patience and confidence. Maybe that's why, without realizing it, she's overly critical of my role in the office. "I hope Aunt Rose stays at home today," I say to myself.

The work is very interesting. I'm learning more than I ever imagined about medicine. I like to read the patients' charts before I take them to the examining room. But more than that, I love working with the patients. Meeting so many new people, listening to their problems, this is right up my alley. I'm not letting Rose intimidate me. She'll be gone soon, busy with her new baby.

Some patients are regulars, like Sylvia Perlman, our favorite hypochondriac. This week she's sure she has a heart condition. Dr. Ben assures her that her pulse and heart rate are normal. She probably has a case of nerves. I've learned just how to handle Mrs. Perlman now. I listen and take notes. Then I make sincere and caring eye contact, and smile. The technique never fails me. I've got it down to a science.

And then we have Mrs. Coppola. *Big* Mrs. Coppola. Her stomach is always bloated, and indigestion plagues her daily. Uncle Ben tries to tell her to change her diet. That's hard to do when you make Sunday sauce with meatballs and sweet sausage each week for the whole family. Weight loss is out of the question, I'm afraid. When her appointment is over, we chat about recipes. She promises to bring a sample of her famous rice pudding next week, when she comes for her follow up appointment.

Today we welcomed a very interesting new patient to our office. His name is Theodore Damsky. He's suffering from back pain, due to scoliosis. He has a nice-looking face, and very kind, intelligent eyes. His body is somewhat crooked, due to the curve and bump on his back, but yet it's not enough to be disfiguring. His quiet demeanor interests me. Perhaps his shyness is due to years of living with an unusual body type. When I take his medical history, he explains the reason for the office visit.

"I've seen many doctors and specialists. They've given me Laudanum for pain. They've even tried traction. Nothing has helped. I've heard great things about Dr. Bader. I'm hoping he can help me."

With a smile, I say "I hope so too. The Doctor will be with you shortly."

When Mr. Damsky's appointment is over, he stops at the front desk to take care of the payment. I make his follow up appointment for next week.

"Just as I expected, Dr. Bader is a fine physician. He feels that he can be of help with my back pain," Mr. Damsky says.

"He usually does help his patients, or so they tell me. You see, Dr. Bader is my uncle. So perhaps I'm biased," I say with a smile. We'll see you next week then, Mr. Damsky."

He responds with a smile, "Please call me Teddy. That's what my friends call me."

"Ok then. Have a safe trip home. It's been a pleasure to meet you." I say, returning Teddy's smile.

"Likewise, Miss....?"

"My name is Mrs. Hannah Altman. I've only been working here a short time."

I don't know why, but I feel a need to open up to this man. I tell him why I must work, about Abe passing away, and about my two children. The words keep coming. I wonder whether I've said too much. But there is something about those kind, intelligent eyes. He smiles, thanks me, and leaves.

# My Saturday Visitor

The weekend is here and as usual, Tessie arrives at 1:00. The tea and rugelach are already on my round kitchen table. Today I decide to put out a pretty yellow flowered table cover to brighten things up. We sit down to talk. The children run in for the usual candy and coins. They say thank you and run back outside to play. Tessie's floral scent overwhelms me. Again, I don't comment. Why insult a good friend? I wonder to myself what the most current drama will be.

Today she wants to vent about her daughter. Alice is a senior in high school. "She's so beautiful, so bright, so dear. Why does she have to have a boyfriend like Joe? He drives a delivery truck. His family has nothing. She could do so much better." Tessie's head is in her hands now. "Little Alvin thinks that Joe is great. He practices magic tricks on him, and Joe plays along. Alvin loves that. Joe gives Alvin a quarter and tells him to 'get out of here kid.' They laugh and give each other a little punch on the shoulder. He's a nice young man Hannah, but not for my Alice."

I pause for a moment before responding. I want to sound reassuring. "I wouldn't worry about it, Tessie. They're young. Let them enjoy their innocent years together. And Little Alvin likes him. Children have a good sense of people. It will work out for the best."

Tessie shakes her head and frowns, "I hope you're right Hannah. But my Alice deserves better. I don't want her to be stuck in a marriage like mine, always struggling. If we didn't have our boarding house, we would have nothing. The small rent we get from our boarders keeps us going. I want Alice's life to be different. Let her have beautiful clothes, a nice house, a big car. Maybe even a maid."

Then the dramatic sigh, followed by a dreamy eyed pause. Tessie looks up at me. "How was your week Hannah? You must be used to that job, are you?"

I think for a moment and reply, "Oh yes Tessie. So much better now. Aunt Rose is home with her new little son, Michael. She's consumed with motherhood, which leaves me to run the office with no one looking over my shoulder. What I love the most is all the people that I meet. Just yesterday, we had a new patient. I proceed to tell her about Mr. Damsky. "He has a rounded back, scoliosis. My uncle will try to find a remedy for his back pain. He's shy and has a very kind face. There is something very interesting about him."

"Hannah, you seem to be *very* interested," she teases me.

"Don't be foolish Tessie. No one could ever replace Abe. I can't imagine ever being interested in another man in that way. But I can have friends, can't I? Both female *and* male. It doesn't matter to me. You know I'm a freethinker and I love getting to know all kinds of people."

With that I get one of Tessie's "looks."

After another hour, Tessie stands up to leave. I'm secretly glad, because I need to spend some time with my children. I hope they don't feel neglected because I work so much now.

"Goodbye Tessie," I say as we embrace, her perfume overwhelming me once again.

I take a little time for myself while the children play on the stoop. When they come in before dinner, I get a big hug from Solly. "I love you, MMMommy."

Frances comes in full of excitement. She was the winner of the Double Dutch contest. Oh, such a joy to see their sweet faces. They smell like a combination of fresh air, sunshine, and sweat.

"Wash up for supper please, you two," I say, lovingly. "Then I need you to set the table, Frances. I want to show you how to make an omelet tonight. We'll have an omelet with a little cottage cheese." Money is tight. We certainly don't eat lavish meals anymore. Luckily, I'm pretty good at stretching a dollar. I don't believe in wasting food, or wasting anything, for that matter.

During supper the children tell me about what's been happening at school. I listen attentively. As I listen, I notice that Solly's stutter is more exaggerated when he speaks fast. I try to slow him down. He smiles and puts his head down. Frances has been working with him on reciting the times tables.

Talking with the children after supper helps me keep my mind away from the melancholy that I feel when I'm alone with my thoughts. Dark thoughts of what my life had been with Abe. His drinking, the way he hid it from me. Why did I choose to ignore it? Could I have helped him? He appeared to have been a happy, contented man, but was he? What makes a man drink like that? Our lives seemed fine, but was I looking at Abe through rose-colored glasses? With hindsight, I'm glad the drinking never became an issue between us. It bubbled under the surface only. Let the happy memories carry me through this dark time, I decide.

# Goldberg's Delicatessen

On my way to work this morning, I can't help but think about a conversation I had with my uncle yesterday. He didn't seem quite like himself. I asked him if he was feeling well?

"Well Hannah, I guess I'm OK. But I *am* concerned about my wife. Rose is crazy about the baby, but she's very intense. When the baby cries, she gets upset, which then makes the baby more upset. I know he's picking up on her emotions, which all babies do."

"I wouldn't worry dear Uncle," I say. "It takes time to be a confident mother. Aunt Rose will figure out the needs and cries of little Michael before you know it. Babies have different cries for different reasons. There is a sleepy cry, a hungry cry, a wet diaper cry, and most important, a gassy stomach cry."

I secretly hope this advice gets back to Aunt Rose.

I've been thinking about my new friend, and my favorite patient in our office, Mr. Damsky. He wants me to call him Teddy, but Uncle Ben likes me to use formal names with the patients. He says it sounds more professional. Mr. Damsky is very pleased with the treatment he's been getting in our office. *The good doctor*, as Mr. Damsky refers to him, is providing some new treatments. He's developed a customized exercise program, combined with a new brace. I'm so happy it's helping.

With each office visit, Mr. Damsky and I have expanded our friendship. Last Thursday, he was the last patient of the day. He asked me to meet him at Goldberg's Delicatessen on the corner after work.

I paused for just a second thinking through the logistics of it, and then said, "Well, let me see about that. I'll have to run home and get the children settled first. They would worry about me if I was late. I'll ask my neighbor, Claire, to look in on the kids."

At 6:00, Teddy and I sat down for a cream soda, a corned beef on rye, and conversation. It was sure to happen, and I was so happy. I knew he would be an interesting man. We had a connection, I could feel it. I kind of need a new friend, I thought. Tessie's wonderful, but Teddy's intelligence intrigues me.

"What kind of work do you do Mr. Damsky, I mean Teddy," I ask with a smile.

"Have you ever heard of *The Jewish Gazette?* It's a small Zionist paper that I started 2 years ago. It's on most of the newsstands, but usually people reach for the *Jewish Daily*

*Forward.* I feel there are enough of our people that we should be able to support more than one Jewish newspaper. Don't you agree?"

"I think you're right. We need more than one point of view. I love *The Forward.* My parents read it, so it was always in my house."

Teddy tells me that next time he comes into the office he'll bring a copy of the *Gazette* for me.

"I'd love to take a look," I say, happy that he thinks enough of me to share his interest. We chat a while longer, until our cream sodas are finished. I love sitting in Goldberg's delicatessen. The tables are so close together that you can listen to the conversations at the tables next to you (which I do). The scent of corned beef and smoked pastrami permeates the air. Half sour pickles, mustard, and cole slaw are on each table.

But, much as I love the delicatessen, I think to myself how nice it would be to do this at home, with hot tea in a glass and my mandel bread for dunking. What would Franny and Solly think? What would the neighbors think? Is it too soon to have a male visitor, even if he is only a friend?

The next day in the office, Ben pulls me aside. "Hannah, I want you to help Rose with the baby. But she can't know that I've asked you. She's a proud woman. When you talked about babies having different cries for different reasons, it occurred to me that Rose may not realize this."

I answered, "I understand, Uncle Ben. I didn't know it either when I first had my own kids. My mother taught me, and with experience, I became aware. I'll try my best to help, and I promise to be discreet. Frances and Solly would love to see their little cousin. We could stop by on Sunday."

# Baby Advice

Frances and Solly can't contain their excitement. They haven't seen little Michael since the *Bris*. And on that day, there was a "no touching" rule. This time, I hope they will be able to hold the baby.

My children have always loved visiting Aunt Rose and Uncle Ben. One day last year, Ben had invited Solly and Frances to come along with him on his house calls. They waited in the big black Desoto while he made his visits. He had a very ill patient, and climbed up five flights of stairs carrying his well-worn black bag to calm the sick child and prescribe medication. Next, he drove to another house for an elderly man with bronchitis. After his house calls were done, he stopped and bought the kids each a sweet potato from the *Sweet Potato Man,* who had a charcoal oven on his pushcart. No wonder they love him so much.

We ring the bell, bearing gifts. The kids wrapped up a rattle that they picked out themselves at Woolworths. I baked some rugelach made with walnuts and raspberry jam.

I'm hoping all his will cheer Aunt Rose up. I remember the stress and loneliness of caring for an infant. It can be hard to be alone for so many hours with a crying baby. Insecurity can haunt you. Combine those emotions with lack of sleep and a new mother can be quite miserable. I hope our visit will serve to make things just a little better.

"Thank you for coming children," Rose says as she opens the door. "Little Michael is just waking up from his nap. Uncle Ben will bring him out to the front parlor. I'm making some tea for us." She takes my plate of rugelach and says, "These will be great with our tea, Hannah, thank you."

I give her a hug.

"I want to hold him, ppplease Mom," says Solly.

"Why don't we let Frances go first. Is that OK Aunt Rose?" Rose seems uneasy, but Uncle Ben gives the OK. Solly and Frances share the honor of holding the baby. Smiles cover their faces. When little Michael starts to fuss, Aunt Rose takes over and goes into the bedroom to nurse her son. But the crying continues. Uncle Ben asks me to set up the tea and cookies, while he helps Rose calm the baby down.

After a few minutes, all is quiet. When the breast feeding is over, we all gather in the kitchen. Rose lets me hold Michael now. He smells so good as I gently rock him in my arms. His little head has that wonderful baby smell. Ahhhh, I love this feeling.

"Babies are the best. I remember my own mother teaching me about different cries, and how to understand and respond to each one," I say carefully, feeling my way into the subject.

Rose frowns. "Nonsense Hannah. A cry is a cry. I know what my child needs. When I want your advice, I'll ask for it. How are things going in the office? Are you doing any better there? I hope you're being professional at all times. My husband's success depends on it, right Ben?"

"We're doing just fine dear. Hannah is a big help, but we both miss you. The patients always ask for you, right Hannah?" I assure Rose that the office runs smoothly. She can't make me nervous anymore. I know what I'm doing and I can tell the patients are comfortable with me.

We spend some more time together, chatting about current events. The economy is so bad that it worries us all, and we hope that President Hoover will be able to help New Yorkers get jobs. Tessie's husband Simon is an example. He has been in and out of work lately. Just putting food on the table is a challenge.

"Let's not take away from our enjoyment of our new little blessing," says Uncle Ben.

The children are teaching Michael how to hold the rattle. Even Aunt Rose seems happy, watching her son clutch and shake his new toy. I take in this family moment. How much sweeter it would be if Abe was here with us now? He always knew how to be the life of the party, full of jokes and good humor. I try to be that person, but it doesn't come naturally to me. *Be who you are Hannah,* I hear Abe say. His support is with me still.

# Recipe for Rugelach

There's something 'sweet' about Rugelach and it's not just the sugar in the recipe. This tiny pastry makes every cup of tea (or coffee) taste better and that makes everyone sitting at the table smile. Rugelach takes some time to make, but it's worth it because it makes your guests and family feel so good. They're perfect for special occasions.

**8 oz. cream cheese**
**8 oz. sweet butter, softened**
**½ cup confectioner's sugar**
**Pinch of salt**
**½ tsp. lemon juice**
**½ tsp. vanilla**
**2 cups flour**
**1 cup apricot or raspberry jam**
**¾ cup chopped walnuts**
**¾ cup sugar**
**1 egg**

Mix cream cheese, butter, confectioner's sugar, salt, lemon juice, and vanilla. Stir in flour. Knead to a very soft dough. Refrigerate 1 hour or more. Divide dough into 2 equal balls. Roll out each ball into ¼ inch thick squares. Smear with jam. Sprinkle with walnuts. Roll each square into a jellyroll and cut into ½ inch pieces. Brush with beaten egg and sprinkle with granulated sugar. Lay flat on greased cookie sheet. Bake in preheated 350-degree oven for 25 minutes. Makes 30 cookies.

# The Newspaper Business

Teddy and I have developed a strong friendship now. After he showed me *The Gazette,* things have changed between us. I am intrigued. I admire this man. Out of nothing but hard work, and a passion for his craft, he has developed an excellent publication. He has a small staff of writers, most of them labor organizers, Zionists, and freethinkers, who are committed to the success of the paper.

"Hannah, I value your opinion. Please be honest with me. Compliments are wonderful, but I need someone who is willing to tell me where I need to change, where I can improve," says Teddy, while we sip our glasses of tea.

This evening we're in my kitchen. Teddy likes my baking, so this time I made a sponge cake for us. I used lots of eggs to make it extra fluffy. It's still warm, since I just took it out of the oven. We feel comfortable being together in my apartment. Frances and Solly like Mommy's new friend. Teddy gives them little treats too, just like Tessie Lester, but without that strong perfume. We visit each week after his back treatment with Uncle Ben. Quite often now, we skip

Goldberg's delicatessen and we walk together to my place. It's become a welcome routine.

"If you want honesty, you'll get honesty. The paper is a little dry. Serious news stories are important. With the Depression going on all around us, people need the truth. Your editorials are insightful. I applaud you for that. But Teddy, people also need a break, a distraction. You know I love *A Bintel Brief.* Why not have an advice column in *The Jewish Gazette*? How about a page just for women? You can also have a poetry column each week. Something for children too. Maybe even puzzles for the mind." I suggest.

Teddy gives me a *look.* "Really? That all seems frivolous to me. Look at this world — anti-Semitism in Europe and here in our own country, labor problems, breadlines. The list is endless. And you want an advice column?"

"You have just made my point Teddy. Some of us mortals need an escape from all that. Why don't you try it? If sales improve at the newsstand, you'll have your answer."

Teddy's expression reveals to me that he'll at least give it some thought. "There's something I haven't told you yet, Hannah. I'm a little embarrassed about it. We're struggling financially. I mean it's serious. The paper's running out of money. I've been supporting this project of mine from savings from my previous business, which was a successful real estate venture. I took a big chance on this paper. So, I think I should give your idea consideration. I'm pretty desperate at this point."

"I'm so sorry to hear that. But you should be proud, even if the work will never make you a rich man. Your paper is still new. There is plenty of time to increase circulation," I say. "Speaking of work, I think we better say goodnight. I need to be fresh for Uncle Ben's office tomorrow morning."

Teddy gets up and we awkwardly walk to the front door. Our hands brush together. I feel my face flush, and that familiar feeling in my body that I haven't felt since Abe died. I wonder if Teddy feels it too.

"Good night, Hannah. I'll see you next week. I'll tell you what my staff says about your ideas," Teddy says with a wink of his eye. We walk out the door together. When I close the door behind me, I feel like a teenager. I don't know what to make of this feeling, but I know I like it.

# Summer Camp

I've decided that Frances and Solly deserve a break this summer. The city bakes in July and August with heat reflecting off the buildings and the pavement. When there is no breeze, it can be oppressive. Sometimes we sleep on the fire escape, just to cool off. A few of the neighborhood kids go to summer camp. Why not my kids? Sure, money is tight, but don't they deserve to go? I must admit, selfishly, I can use a break too. It will be good for everyone, I decide.

Camp "Garden of Eden" seems perfect. I read about it in *The Jewish Daily Forward,* which subsidizes the camp for city kids. The community is concerned about the poor health conditions of Jewish city children. *The Forward* has always taken on the cause of the underprivileged. If I apply and if we're accepted, the fee will only be $10 for 2 weeks. The paper informs the readership where to apply. After I fill out a long application, I submit it, with fingers crossed and a few weeks later I receive a letter. We've been accepted for the last session— the last two weeks in August, right before school is to begin in the fall.

I thought Frances and Solly would be thrilled, but instead, they frown, and the "what ifs" begin. "What if the counselors beat us at night? What if we get homesick? What if we hate the food? What if I get sick? What if there are dangerous animals in the woods?"

I tell them not to worry, that it will be fun, but this is their first time out of the city on their own and they're uneasy. Frances will be a Junior Counselor, helping the Senior Counselor, but she's unsure about her responsibilities. Solly doesn't admit to being afraid. He's always up for an adventure. Maybe because he's a boy, and a little younger, a little naive.

I hope the children at camp won't tease Solly because of his stutter. Frances won't always be there to protect him. She'll be in her own bunk. I put these thoughts aside, and decide to put a positive spin on the concept of camping.

"You will enjoy the fresh air, the arts and crafts, and the plays," I tell them.

Frances reads aloud from the pamphlet about the camp. The organization that runs the camp believes in teaching the children Yiddish, and there will be discussions, songs and plays about labor unions and socialism. I hope all this won't be too extreme, I say to myself.

The day arrives for departure. We take a train and a ferry to get to Newburgh, New York. Right away the kids are greeted by friendly teenage counselors. My two children surprise me.

They smile and say goodbye without a fuss. I'm relieved. I'm glad Tessie will be visiting tomorrow. It will distract me from missing my little ones.

My sleep was fitful that night. Although I was physically exhausted from the trip to Newburgh, my mind was racing with worrisome fears and thoughts. *Calm down Hannah*, I think. I should be pleased. Kids in camp, a job that pays the rent, friendships, old and new.

"We are lucky Hannah," I imagine Abe saying. He knew how to be positive about life. In the evenings, when I can't sleep, Abe comes to me in my thoughts. I welcome him with great love and relief. It's almost like he's still here.

I wake up early and take out the ingredients for my mandel bread. Walnuts, butter, flour, sugar … pretty soon my kitchen smells like heaven. I make a cup of coffee and sit down to wait for the mandel bread to come out of the oven. Tessie Lester will be here soon. So much to talk about.

The doorbell rings at 12:30. "Tessie's early today," I think. As I open the door and prepare myself for the scent of Evening in Paris, I'm surprised to see my new friend, Teddy Damsky. He's carrying a newspaper.

"I hope I'm not intruding, but I was passing by and decided I wanted to see you. Here Hannah, I brought you today's paper. Maybe we can talk some more about your ideas. My colleagues liked some of them."

I try to disguise my excitement, but I can feel my face flush a little. I hope Teddy doesn't notice. I invite him in to sit down and have something to eat. Our hands come together at the table. Teddy looks up at me. My eyes meet his and then I look down, unsure of what to do or think. Our relationship is somewhat professional, and we should try to keep it on that level. But we both know something very special is happening. People like Teddy Damsky don't come around very often. I don't want to lose this new and wonderful relationship.

Just then the doorbell rings again. This time it's Tessie, in all her glory. Well, I guess it's time for my two friends to meet.

"Is someone here Hannah?" I quietly explain that Teddy has stopped by. Tessie has no intention of leaving. That's not her style. She walks right up to Teddy and puts out her hand to introduce herself. "A pleasure to meet you. I've heard all about you Mr. Damsky."

"Likewise, I'm sure," says Teddy. Conversation always comes easily with Tessie around. She speaks to Teddy freely with complaints about Simon's lack of a job, a boarder who is late with the rent, and Alvin's teacher who doesn't appreciate his genius abilities. "He's a creative dreamer who is above the other children, so he's bored."

"And what do you do Mr. Damsky?" Teddy takes a minute to answer her.

"Let's just say I own a struggling newspaper. Hannah has offered to help me with it," he says.

"I'd be happy to help too," Tessie replies. "And my husband Simon too. It seems like he's *always* looking for a job. Maybe he could help you out in some way. He's not a journalist, but he's very good with his hands, with machines. He can fix anything."

"I'll be sure to keep that in mind Tessie. Now I think it's time for me to go, but it was a pleasure to meet you. Hannah, I'll see you later in the week at Dr. Bader's office."

When he leaves I explain to Tessie about the scoliosis. She says she notices his back, that it's lightly rounded. "But those eyes," Tessie says. "When he looks at you Hannah, something happens in those eyes. Do you think it's a little soon to have a male friend? Abe hasn't even been gone a year. How does it look? A *shonda* maybe?" I stop for a moment to think about that.

"Maybe Tessie. Just maybe. But he is truly a good friend. We have a common interest, the newspaper. And I need that right now. It feels right."

We embrace as Tessie leaves to head home. As evening comes, I settle down with the copy of *The Jewish Gazette* that Teddy brought me. I compare it to *The Jewish Daily Forward.* Although both are Jewish publications, the *Forward* is written in Yiddish, so that the new immigrants can read it. The *Forward* grew out of the Labor and Socialist movement. But the *Gazette* is a newer paper, more modern. It's written in English, with a little Yiddish here and there. *The Gazette* focuses on the Jewish dream, Zionism, as well as political events in Europe and the US.

I take some notes to give to Teddy when I see him. I have a strong feeling that I can add to his newspaper. Why hire a stranger, when I'm almost an expert on *A Bintel Brief?* I read the column faithfully. I bet I could start an advice column for him. A surge of confidence sweeps through my body. I sit up straighter. If I can work alongside Teddy, we will be sure to spend more time together. The more I think about that idea, the more I like it.

I decide to be a little pushy for a change. Why not show Teddy that my idea could really work? So, I write an ad to be placed in *The Jewish Gazette* to solicit advice letters. Of course, we can't call it *A Bintel Brief.* That name is taken. But how about *Help Me Hannah?* I like the sound of it.

*Attention Dear Readers.*

*The Jewish Gazette will be starting a new feature: An advice column just for you. Send us your problems, your woes, your dilemmas. Our staff can help. Send your letter, attention:* **Help Me Hannah**. *If chosen, your letter will appear in our publication, with a helpful answer. All names will remain confidential.*

# The Show Must Go On

The two weeks of camp seem endless. My eerily quiet apartment is perfectly clean and neat. I never thought I would miss all the noise and the extra work that children bring. Eating supper alone while listening to my favorite radio programs helps pass the time. I now have time to think and to plan for my very own advice column, that is, of course, if Teddy and his staff approve.

On Thursday night, Teddy and I go to Goldberg's delicatessen on the corner after work. This time Teddy says, "Let's treat ourselves to a pastrami sandwich, with a half sour pickle. We can wash it down with a cream soda." We both eat with great hunger and enthusiasm, having worked hard all day. The tartness of the mustard, the sour taste of this pickle.....we eat with such delight that it makes us both laugh a little. The sandwich is so big that I can hardly open my mouth wide enough. "We must look like two starving children," I say with a smile.

"How are the children doing at camp?" Teddy asks, between bites. I tell him that I've received a few letters, and that they sounded happy. What a relief.

"On the final Sunday of camp, when the children are to be picked up, there's a special event planned. Both Frances and Solly will be participating in a play for the parents and the campers. Franny tells me in her letter that she has been helping to make the costumes. She'll work behind the curtain helping with costume changes. But I'm shocked to learn that Solly has a very big speaking part. I'm really looking forward to seeing it," I tell Teddy.

"Well, how would you like some company? I love the theatre. I'm sure the production at Camp Garden of Eden will be as good as any Broadway show. Or maybe the Yiddish theater is more like it," Teddy teases.

"Teddy. Do you really want to spend a Sunday traveling to Newburgh and watch my kids perform? I would love the company, but I don't want to impose on your free time."

"Hannah, being with you and your children is a pleasure for me, always. Because of my condition, I never really considered having a family of my own. Perhaps I lost my confidence with women. When I was a child, kids would tease me in school, called me a hunchback. I lost my dating years. When I became an adult, I would throw myself into projects, business ideas, and now, of course, *The Jewish Gazette*. When I see you with Frances and Solly, I realize how much I've missed."

"But just look at all you've accomplished, Teddy. You should feel proud of that." This is a good time to show

Teddy my proposal for *Help Me Hannah*. I read him the ad that I wrote.

"I'm glad you had this idea Hannah. Your ad is perfect. We'll run with it next week."

I'm relieved and pleased. Now, I tell myself, no turning back, Hannah. You started something, now make it happen.

"Why don't I pick you up at 8:00? We can travel together." I explain about the train, and the ferry, the long and tedious trip. "It will be fun Hannah. See you Sunday."

As we arrive at Camp Garden of Eden, I notice that the sun is shining brightly, with a few clouds in the sky, making that sun even more appreciated. The air smells like freshly cut grass.

My heart races at the prospect of seeing my kids. They're waiting for me at the entrance. We hug as if it's been two years, not two weeks.

"Look kids, I brought a special guest today. Do you remember Mr. Damsky?" They say yes, shyly. Teddy puts them at ease. "When your mother told me about the play, I knew I had to see it."

There's an announcement on the loud speaker, telling parents to go to the **Theatre Shed** at 2:00. "Campers go to your bunks to put on costumes, prepare for the show."

We decide to go early to get good seats for the performance. As we stroll through the grassy path, Teddy grabs my hand as we walk together. *The Theatre Shed* is a large, dilapidated three-sided structure, like an amateur version of an open-air theatre.

For Teddy and me, it feels very natural to be close at this moment. As we take our seats, I'm excited and a little nervous. I'm sure Frances will be fine. She has become a very poised young lady. But Solly? A major role, with his stutter? Butterflies are dancing in my stomach.

The curtain opens and the announcer introduces the show, which is called, The *Internationale*. *"Arise ye workers from your slumbers...."* The children are singing, in their loudest voices, the theme song of the Labor/Socialist movement.

Frances is busy backstage. Ten-year old Solly, to our surprise, plays the evil owner of the factory. He's dressed in a black top hat and coat, with gold dollar signs on his back and front. He recites a long monologue in Yiddish, mixed with some English. He delivers his lines with great expression as a true villain. He fears that the strikers will shut down his factory. The workers march across the stage, with picket signs, and they recite over and over again: *The bosses, the bosses, they make us work like horses.*

When the play is over, during the curtain call, Frances and Solly come out beaming. Solly's performance was stellar. And no stutter, *none*. I am amazed.

The audience claps and gives a standing ovation. I run to the stage to hug my little actor and my costume designer. What a wonderful way to end two great weeks in Camp Garden of Eden. Teddy and I, along with tired, but happy Frances and Solly, begin our journey back to the city. Fresh air from the country fills our lungs. The heat and grime of Washington Heights awaits us, but for now, we're all aglow.

# Part 2: Branching Out

## Help Me Hannah

Saturday arrives. Today Tessie brings Alvin along to play with Solly. Little skinny Alvin with his shiny black hair and big blue eyes. He shows me a magic trick with cards. "Wow, how did you do that Alvin?"

With a twinkle in his eye, he says, "Magic, Mrs. Altman, just plain old magic."

I have so much to tell Tessie. For a change, I've made Mrs. Cappola's famous rice pudding instead of my usual mandel bread. Last time she came to the office for her dyspepsia, she brought in a generous sample for the Doctor and the recipe for me. We all sit down for a taste, even the children. Everyone loves their cold, creamy bowl of pudding.

"Can we go out and play now, Mrs. Altman?" asks Alvin. The two boys run outside with the *Spauldeen* ball in Solly's hand. Stickball is the plan, I guess. Frances slept late this morning, but she goes out too, to meet her friends from the neighborhood. *"Zie Gezunt* kids, be careful out there," Tessie says.

Tessie tells me that Simon got a new job. "He's working in a factory that makes ladies vanity sets. You know Hannah: brushes, combs, matching mirrors. For rich ladies who have a vanity table in their bedrooms. He brought a set home for me as a present. I have a feeling he snuck it out. If he gets caught stealing…...here we go again. The man doesn't use his head. Where is his *Yiddishe Kup*? Maybe he wasn't born with one!"

I try to listen without commenting. Tessie doesn't need any harsh words or judgement right now. Luckily, I know her boarding house income will be just enough to keep food on the table, in case Simon loses this job too. I put my hand on hers, hoping my touch will soothe her worries.

I tell Tessie all about the camp, the play, and how Teddy came with me for the day and to help me take the children home. She was surprised to hear about Solly's leading role, and that he didn't stutter. "Maybe this means he's outgrowing it," she says.

"From your mouth to God's ears Tessie," I say.

"How is your work going in the doctor's office, Hannah? You must almost be a real nurse by now," she teases.

"Very well, Tessie. I'm learning about many diseases. But most patients come in for common problems, like a cough, a cold, or dyspepsia. It's more interesting when they have a rare complaint, and Uncle Ben is able to diagnose it. Sometimes he discusses the medical aspects with me, and I love that. He knows he can trust me to keep things confidential."

"But I have something even more interesting to tell you. My friend, Teddy Damsky, the newspaper man—I've given him an idea and he likes it. There will be a new feature for *The Jewish Gazette* called *Help Me Hannah*. It's an advice column. Teddy put in the ad to solicit letters and he was flooded with them. I'm going to submit the first question and answer this week. I've been working on it evenings after the children are in bed. I have to choose a good letter. I want the first one to be a very interesting problem, so that we'll continue to receive more. I want the questions to be fascinating to the readers, something that might remind them of their own lives." I say with a cautious smile.

"That sounds very exciting Hannah. A nurse, an advice columnist. I can't keep up with you. Teddy must be a wonderful man to take an interest in your children. And now, with this column, maybe he'll hire you to work at the paper," she says.

"This paper doesn't have the money for that now. But I love helping Teddy and he says if circulation grows, perhaps he will be able to pay me a little something for my time. It would be great, but I won't count on it. We're squeaking by, with insurance checks and my job."

Then I add, "I'm a little concerned about Frances, Tessie. Ever since she's come home from camp, she's been tired all the time. Yesterday she fell down at school. I may ask Uncle Ben if he can make a house call. I'll bribe him with some rice pudding."

Tessie wants to see a *Help Me Hannah* letter. But I tell her she has to buy *The Jewish Gazette* if she wants to see it. "We need to sell newspapers," I say. Tessie tells me she'll buy it from the newsstand around the corner on St. Nicholas Avenue. "I like the blind newsstand owner. He trusts people to put the coins in his tin box. He hears the jingle and knows that we've paid. I like to support him," says Tessie.

Tessie and I go outside to round up the kids. I notice Frances sitting on the stoop. I ask her what's wrong. "I have a headache, Ma." Very unusual for her. Maybe she is still tired from the weeks away at camp.

# Help Me Hannah # 1

*Dear Hannah,*

*When I read about your advice section, I felt that it was a sign for me. I need to unburden myself of this sadness that has overtaken my family.*

*My husband and I arrived at Ellis Island five years ago, from Poland. HIAS helped us to find an apartment. We were doing well and we were happy. We now have a baby boy and I am pregnant. We both went to night school to learn English. My husband worked in a factory that makes children's pajamas. But he lost that job, and these days it's hard to find another one.*

*He has been going door to door to ask for odd jobs from the people on our street. He says he will paint, clean up, fix things for them. A few kind people have given him a small job, like painting a bathroom, or cleaning a rusty radiator, and paid him a dollar.*

*Sometimes, I go to the butcher to ask for scraps of liver "for the cat" I say. I'm ashamed to admit it's for us. But those were the good days. Now we really have nothing. For dinner last night, the three of us sat at the table and my husband took out of his pocket a bag of green grapes. He gave us each one, then another, dealing them out like a deck of cards. My son got the last extra grape. We tried to act normal, but then my husband put his head in his hands and sobbed.*

*I'm afraid he's losing confidence and hope. He has always been a proud man. I love my husband and hate to see him this way.*

*What are we to do?*

*Respectfully,*

*Hungry and concerned*

· · · · · · ·

*Dear Hungry and concerned,*

*You are a brave and caring wife. Your husband is a good man who is trying his best in a nearly impossible situation. And you are not alone, just look at the bread lines all over our city.*

*My advice is:*

1. *Your dear husband must continue to do his odd jobs. Perhaps one will lead to permanent employment.*
2. *Look in the Help Wanted section in The Jewish Gazette. Have your husband apply for work. He can't be picky either.*
3. *If any of our fine readers can find it in their hearts to help this family, please contact our newspaper (attention: Help Me Hannah). We can introduce you with the hope that you will be able to employ this worthy man.*
4. *Don't be afraid to ask for help. HLAS and the UJA are good organizations for you to seek assistance.*

*Most of all, do not give up hope. You both must hold your heads high. Stay strong and stay focused. Praise your husband for his effort. Never let him feel like a failure. Good things come to those who work hard in The United States of America.*

# A Diagnosis

When I wake the children for school today, Frances seems to have trouble getting out of bed. "Stay home today, Frances. I want Uncle Ben to see you." I walk Solly to school and then I walk to work. I want to tell my uncle about Frances. When I do, he looks concerned. During lunch, he walks home with me to see my daughter. He examines her and asks her to walk across the room. She struggles to move her legs. She has a fever of 103.4. My heart sinks.

"Hannah, stay home this afternoon with your daughter. She needs you. I'm concerned that Frances may have contracted Poliomyelitis from the swimming pool at camp. We must act quickly, just in case. Solly should go to stay with your parents in Bridgeport. Polio is highly contagious. I want you to arrange this instantly," he tells me.

Without explaining too much to Solly, I arrange for my parents to take him. He'll be well taken care of by my extended family in Bridgeport. I need to focus on my dear daughter. She needs me now.......full time, full attention.

Rose makes some arrangements for a baby sitter for her son, Michael, so that she can fill my shoes in the office. What a reversal. I know how concerned she must be for my Franny. That scares me even more.

Uncle Ben acts quickly. Before I know it, we have a quarantine sign on the door. My wonderful uncle sits me down for "the talk." I listen with all my attention, while trying to stay calm.

"Hannah, I want to be honest with you. Let's start with the worst circumstance. If Frances has a severe case of polio, she may lose use of her legs. Her breathing may be affected also. The medical community has some promising new treatments. We have the iron lung. Sister Kenney from Australia has developed a set of exercises and massage techniques for the muscles. The best thing I can tell you is that 95% of all cases are very mild, with full recovery. We caught this one early. I have every reason to believe that your little girl will pull through. But you should know how important it is to be vigilant. Do you understand?"

"Of course, Uncle. I'm ready to do what must be done."

For the next month, I stay home with Frances. We treat her fever, and thankfully it returns to normal in two days. Uncle Ben has given me exercises to strengthen her legs, and we practice these daily. I put hot compresses on her legs three times a day. Uncle Ben stops by to check on us. He's pleased with the progress. Because he has influence in the medical community, he is able to keep Frances from going to the hospital. We promise to isolate in quarantine. My uncle visits daily, monitoring her symptoms and oversees the strengthening exercises. He watches Franny walk with help across the room and we both see progress. I am encouraged.

A month goes by. I can't bear the thought of my daughter in an iron lung, or needing braces to walk, like so many other children I have seen. I won't let myself think about losing her.

To keep Frances distracted we delve into reading. We reread some of her favorite Nancy Drew mysteries. If she feels too weak, I read to her. It helps pass the time. Abe used to read to the children each night. He was their favorite story teller. Now I'm happy to take over that role. Together we read the new Pearl Buck novel. I think my daughter is ready for grown up books.

Reading distracts us both from the horror that might be. I believe that stress and worry might harm Franny's immune system. I want her thoughts to be of things other than medicines and therapies.

In the evenings we like to gather around the big radio in our parlor and listen to *The Eddie Cantor Show,* Fred Allen, and of course *The Rise of the Goldbergs.* Oh, how I love that Molly Goldberg. Franny does too.

One day, Frances says, "Mom, I hate being sick. But I love being alone with you all day. I miss you when you're at work. I feel too young to take care of Solly and to prepare supper for us."

This statement feels like a knife in my heart, but I don't show her how it hurts. "I need to work, Franny. Rent is expensive. Someday I know you'll understand."

I try to think of more things to distract Franny. We need activities that don't involve using her lower body. I have some scrap materials for hat making, which I haven't touched in over a year. I was pretty good in my day. A few green feathers, some felt, beads - I teach her how to sketch out a hat design, and then slowly craft that design into a finished product. I tell myself to get some more materials for hat making.

I make Franny chicken soup with kreplach. The meat inside those little dumplings will give her much needed iron. She eats very little, but with each day, I see her appetite improving. The hot clear broth contains vitamins from the carrots and celery. And then, of course, my mandel bread always cheers her up.

Teddy has been concerned about Franny and about me. He stays in touch with me and wants to help. I tell him I need to devote my time to Frances. I can't see him now, but I appreciate his kindness. This man has proven his fine character to me over and over again.

Uncle Ben examined Franny for the hundredth time and is pleased with her continuing progress. "I think we've conquered this awful disease, Hannah. With love, and a lot of help from God, your Frances will be fine. Let's wait a few more weeks to bring Solly back home. You can slowly resume your life. But let's delay your return to work. We need to keep Frances home and resting."

As I resume my life, I take on another Help Me Hannah letter. Teddy has printed one each week in *The Jewish Gazette*. I was able to work on them from home. Teddy met me outside on the street, and then brought them to his office. With a big smile he tells me that they appear to be very popular. Today's letter is one that I have spent much time thinking about. How shall I advise this poor, smitten, but confused young man?

# Help Me Hannah # 2

*Please Help Me Hannah,*

*A funeral. That's where it all began. Last month my brother Max and I attended a funeral of a "landsman" from our hometown in Hungary. Standing before me was a beautiful woman. She had a full figure, jet black curly hair, and dazzling green eyes. When she spoke she almost sounded like a real American, I still sound like a greenhorn. Our eyes met and it felt like electricity shot through my whole body. Unfortunately, my brother Max felt the same way.*

*This woman, I will call her "Sylvia", flirted with both of us. She went on a date with me one night, and with my brother the next. We are both in love with her. We both sent her flowers, gifts, and candy. But she said she liked me best. I asked Sylvia to marry me and she said yes.*

*I brought her home to meet my mother. When Max saw us, he became angry. We argued and Max punched me. I defended myself. My poor mother screamed and separated us. But it was too late. I left Max bloodied on the floor. Sylvia and I left. When I came home my mother asked how I could think of marrying a woman who would play one brother against the other? A woman who would break up a family? Now my family won't speak to me. My brother Max looks at me with fury in his eyes.*

*I love Sylvia very much. We want to marry. Maybe meeting at a funeral was a bad omen. I cannot let her go. Hannah, please guide me.*

*Confused*

• • • • • • •

*Dear Confused,*

*You must be very careful. Do not rush into a marriage with a woman who your mother warns against. Your mother loves you and she loves your brother. She has had life experience. You are still young and infatuated. Ask yourself if you're thinking clearly. Listen to your intuition. Don't make any decisions until you know for sure that you can trust this very captivating but conniving young woman.*

# Drive to Bridgeport

Saturday comes without a visit from Tessie. She's afraid of the polio virus, even though my Frances is fine now. The contagion is no longer with us, the quarantine sign is off the front door. But I understand how she feels. "We'll get together again when all this settles, Tessie." I hope my daughter doesn't become an outcast. I will do everything in my power to make sure that doesn't happen.

"Don't worry Hannah. People, even me, have a fear of the unknown. Let's wait a few weeks. Let Franny get strong. No harm in being careful," Tessie tells me.

Frances and I spend this Saturday reading, me —*The Jewish Gazette* and Frances — her favorite, *Nancy Drew*, and we listen to our radio programs. We love *The Eddie Cantor Show*. Franny loves *Little Orphan Annie*. While she's engrossed in her story, I heat up last night's chicken fricassee for supper. We never seem to get tired of chicken fricassee, with its creamy rice and soft chicken that falls off the bone.

"Frances, you have shown so much improvement, tomorrow you'll have a day off. We won't do any exercises or massage. We are going to pick up your brother," I tell her. "It's time for us all to be together again."

Teddy has offered to drive us. Uncle Ben says we can use his DeSoto. We'll take a ride to Bridgeport. I look forward to seeing my parents, brother and sister-in-law, and most of all, Solly. It's been a few months, the longest time we have ever been separated.

As we start our drive, me in the front with Teddy, Franny spread out in the back, he tells me about his problems with the paper. "Circulation is up, but ad sales are down. The two go hand in hand, Hannah," Teddy explains. "A publication like mine needs ad revenue. And you can't generate that revenue unless you can demonstrate that you have a large readership."

"And you get those advertisers how….?" I ask.

"We have staff for that. They work on commission. And they need to have good numbers to convince the businesses that plenty of people will read those ads. Maybe they're not working hard enough. I just don't know."

"If the circulation is up, maybe the ad salesmen will be able to get more advertisers. I know you're working on that."

Before I know it, we're on Whitney Avenue, rounding the corner to my parents' three family house. My brother's family lives on the first floor. Their little son Jeffrey is the light of their lives. My parents are upstairs. There is a renter on the top floor.

When we walk in, my whole body relaxes as we embrace. The reunion brings tears to my eyes. I'm not used to handling big problems alone.

I become a child once again in my mother's arms. When Mama hugs Frances she says, "*OY mein shayna maidele*, am I glad to see you. Let me watch you walk." Frances proudly walks for her, "steady, steady, steady," I say to myself. Although Franny still has a slight limp, she walks with confidence. "Such a relief," says my mother.

"Bubbie, what were you worried about? I'm a fighter," says Franny.

I'm bursting with pride now.

We sit in the front room as I introduce Teddy to the family. After we talk for a while, my mother pulls me aside. "*Nu*, what is this all about Hannah? Mr. Damsky seems like a nice man, but Abe hasn't been gone a year yet."

"I know Mama. I feel the same way. Our friendship 'just happened'. Teddy is kind and caring. The children love him. We're good friends, that's all."

"Hannah, that friendship won't last forever. A man and a woman .... well men need more. But for now, be careful. *Yentas* can be cruel. You deserve to be happy, darling. If you're smart, you will follow your heart, but still be careful."

At that moment, I brought out my mandolin. Each time I visit my parents, they ask me to play, so I decided to bring it with me today. It goes back to the "old days". Every Jewish family tries to provide music lessons for their children, and my parents were no exception. If you could afford a piano, that was ideal. Others, like my family, had to save every penny. We learned accordion, harmonica, or ukulele. In my case it was the mandolin.

We sit around the front room and sing our songs, *Tumbala Laika, My Yiddishe Mama, Raisins and Almonds,* and of course Molly Malone....*cockles and muscles alive alive - o.* Our Irish neighbors taught me that one. Even Teddy joins in the singing. He surprises me. I thought he would be too self - conscious. I give him a pleased smile. I receive a subtle wink in return.

When it comes time to start our drive home, my mother gives me a package. It contains a chicken and a big piece of flanken from the butcher shop. "For you to make a hearty soup Hannah, like I taught you. It will nourish our girl and keep her strong. I'm hoping those vitamins go right to those weak legs of hers." *From your mouth to God's ears.*

"Mmmmom, can I sit up front with you and Mr. DDDDamsky?" Solly asks. "Not today honey. Stay in back with your sister. She's missed you." I'm disappointed that Sol's stutter is back. Frances told me that a schoolmate told her that when Solly recites his times tables at school, he is able to get through them perfectly. It seems that Solly "the entertainer" doesn't stutter at all.

"Ah, it's good to be together again," I say with genuine enthusiasm. For a moment I forget that we're not really together, Abe isn't with us. A strange feeling comes over me. I must be moving on, and I guess that's all right after all.

At home at last, I take a look at the new advice letter that Teddy has given me.

# Help Me Hannah # 3

*Hannah, I am asking you to help me decide how to handle a delicate problem in my family. I have lived in The United States for five years now. I have opened up my small apartment in Brooklyn to my father's Aunt Mollie. She's an old, very religious woman who wears a wig, a sheitel. She is strictly kosher and we are only kosher in "spirit." She disapproves of the way we eat. She cooks and eats her own food. There's a little tension, but we love Aunt Mollie and are happy to help. Mostly, she stays to herself.*

*Aunt Mollie's husband came to New York eight years ago. He sent a steamship ticket for her two years later. But Mollie feared the travel, concerned about being on the ship during the Sabbath. She procrastinated until now. As years passed, the letters stopped coming.*

*Now she is here and wants me to find her husband. I had heard that he had a tailor business in New York. I looked in telephone books and Jewish societies to find Uncle Hershel Cohen. Finally, I hired a detective. Hershel was found in San Francisco. He owns a small tailor shop and has a new wife and two small children.*

*My heart wouldn't allow me to tell Aunt Mollie the truth. So I told her that the detective looked for her husband from one end of the country to the other. He concluded that there is no Hershel Cohen in this country.*

*Aunt Mollie sobbed. She really lost her husband years ago. Now she lost her dream. I took her to synagogue, dressed in black, to recite kaddish for him.*

79

*Did I do the right thing? I am plagued with guilt over this.*

*Sad in Brooklyn*

• • • • • • •

*Dear Sad in Brooklyn,*

*You are obviously a very loving and sensitive nephew. If you had told your aunt the truth, you would have crushed her dreams. Perhaps your aunt suspected the worst. You saved her the shame and humiliation. You trusted your heart. You most certainly did an act of kindness. I applaud your decision.*

# Recipe for Chicken Fricassee

This dish goes a long way. Serve to a large group. Leftovers taste great too. You can use all parts of the chicken, even the gizzards. No wasted food in our family. Serve with rice or potatoes. I prefer rice.

**Ingredients:**

**1 pound of ground beef**

**½ cup bread crumbs or matzoh meal**

**1 egg**

**2 T oil or chicken fat**

**12 chicken wings**

**1 lb chicken gizzards**

**3 sliced onions**

**1 T paprika**

**Salt and pepper**

**2 cup water**

**4 carrots cut into small pieces**

**2 potatoes (optional) cut into small pieces (potatoes not necessary if serving with rice)**

Preheat oven to 300 degrees. Make very small meatballs using first 4 ingredients. Fry or bake them until done. Set aside. Pour oil in large fry pan. Saute chicken wings over medium to high heat until golden brown. Saute a few at a time. Don't crowd the pan. Take out of pan and set aside.Add gizzards to the pan and cook until browned. Remove and set aside.

Add sliced onions to the pan and fry about 5 minutes. Keep stirring until soft.

Now, in a very large casserole dish, add meatballs, gizzards, and wings. Put onions on top. Sprinkle paprika, salt and pepper. You can layer these ingredients. Pout 2 cups water over all of the above. Cover and bake for 45 – 60 minutes. Be sure all meats and vegetables are tender.

# Freida and Golda

With the children settled back in school, I'm able to return to Uncle Ben's office again. Aunt Rose is relieved. Although she had a good nanny for the baby, she prefers being home. She saw that I was able to run the office without her, but, of course, she would never tell me that. Uncle Ben greets me with a hug. "Welcome back Hannah. The patients missed you and so did I."

Today, I welcomed a new patient. She is the cousin of Mrs. Katz, one of our "regulars." Her name is Frieda, and she has just arrived from Austria. She is a beautiful teen, with light brown hair and hazel eyes. Her skin is peaches and cream in color. As I take her medical history, I sense that she has a nervous disorder of some kind and she has a bright red rash on her torso. Later, Uncle Ben pulls me aside to tell me to book a double appointment for Freida next time. "Hannah, she has been through a terrible trauma. Her family has been harassed in Vienna, and her parents sent her here in the hopes of a better life. Their hope is that once she gets settled in NY, she will be able to bring her parents to join her at a later time. She tells me that she's an artist."

"Hannah, what she told me is frightening. I've heard about the problems for the Jews in Europe, but to learn about them first-hand is disturbing. The rumors are true. *The Forward* is trying to bring us current information. We must all be informed. If there ever was a call for Zionism, the time is now."

I shuddered as I thought about what Uncle Ben just said. "It's so upsetting, dear Uncle. We're so lucky to live in the United States. Teddy and I talk about the problems all the time. In fact, he has an interview scheduled with a representative from Tel Aviv. She has just arrived in New York. She's here to do some fundraising for the cause. Teddy invited me to join him for the interview.

"Please keep me informed Hannah," said Uncle Ben. "I want to help. You know we have cousins in Vilna. From the letters I receive from cousin Issac, I have learned that there are nightly anti-Semitic attacks….more pogroms. Will we ever be free of them? Now Jews are being blamed for the economic downturn ...all over Europe. Our people need a homeland. It brings me back to all those hours we spent at the Harlem Zionist Association."

The next Wednesday afternoon, Teddy and I go to the offices of *The Gazette*. Aunt Rose takes over for me at the office that day. There, we meet with a strong, well-spoken woman named Golda Meir. She wears her wavy hair parted in the middle, and pulled back into a bun. Golda has a quiet strength about her. She and her husband have spent the last few years working on a kibbutz. I am mesmerized by her intellect and devotion to the Jewish people.

She asked if we could give her a forum, besides the newspaper interview, with a group of people who might be interested in helping. "Of course, we will," I replied, remembering again, our old group of friends from the Harlem Zionist group.

"I have the perfect spot for our meeting. My Uncle Ben and Aunt Rose, if they're willing, have a large front room and dining room, Mrs. Meir," I say with enthusiasm.

"Please call me Golda, everyone does. And yes, that sounds perfect," she smiles.

"Besides my old Zionist group, let's invite Mrs. Katz and her cousin Freida. If she's not too shy, it would be interesting to hear her reports of Jewish life in Austria," I suggest to Teddy.

"If we publicize the event in my newspaper, our turnout could be impressive," Teddy interjects.

"Well, I think I have enough material for the article about your mission. I'll have one of my writers work with me to finalize it. Thank you for your time, Golda," says Teddy as he puts out his hand.

When Golda leaves, I sense her courage and feel a deep respect for her. "Teddy, when I see a woman like that, it gives me hope that maybe I can accomplish something in this little world of mine. I'm so glad you asked me to write the advice column," I say, hoping for approval.

"*Help Me Hannah* has been a wonderful addition to *The Gazette*. People love it; our circulation is up. And we get so many letters now, as you know." Teddy smiles and leans toward me, puts his hand on my arm. I feel a shot of warmth going through my body. I wonder if he feels it too. I even like the way he smells, clean laundry, soap, aftershave? Whatever it is, I like it. I want to linger.

We both try to be professional, but I'd love our relationship to progress to another level. But how? I feel as if Teddy is reluctant to move forward. I keep thinking about what he said about kids teasing him because of his back. He's such a nice looking man, dark brown eyes, thick wavy hair, warm smile. He's not very tall, but yet he commands respect. It seems so sad that he gave up on living a full life, on having a family. I want to understand more about Teddy's past. I wonder if he knows that there can be so much more to his life. And I want to be a part of it.

# Fundraising

The meeting with Golda was a great success, and her push for a Zionist state was met with enthusiasm. My dear uncle and aunt opened their home, which overflowed with *landsmen*, friends, and interested neighbors. Fundraising goals were met and exceeded.

Golda stood up with confidence when she began to speak. She was wearing a simple black dress with sensible shoes. Her hair was neatly pulled back at the nape of her neck. She spoke in a clear, sincere voice about her life in Tel Aviv. She explained that she and her husband Morris lived and worked on a kibbutz with their children in the Jezreel Valley. Her stories were, perhaps, romanticized, but they were effective. Although life was hard, she loved living off the land, eating wonderful vegetables and fruits from the farm. She talked about evenings of dancing the hora, friendship and love. Franny said to me, "Mom, I want to live on a kibbutz when I'm older."

Frieda Katz walked to the front of the room dressed in a blue skirt and a white sweater. Although she appeared shy and nervous at first, that changed. Once she had the audience listening to her, her young face was able to hide the travails she had already encountered in her life. As she faced the crowd, Frieda seemed hesitant, as if retelling her story would cause her to actually relive it. At first, she spoke in a very soft voice describing the growing anti-Semitism in Austria and the fear that gripped her community there. But as she answered questions, her voice became stronger. She showed us some of her artwork that depicted life in the Jewish ghetto.

Golda stood next to Frieda and tied her story about the growing dangers in Europe to the importance of establishing a Jewish homeland. "Life isn't always easy in Israel. We have a long way to go, and many hurdles. The British and the Arab communities will stand in our way. We need your help. We need hospitals, housing, transportation, weapons." Golda is a forceful speaker and the money collected will go far.

Tessie had come to the meeting, and as usual, was unafraid to voice her opinion. In a strong, accented voice, she said, "I would like to help you with your mission, Mrs. Meir. I will be happy to host another meeting for you to speak to the Jewish community in my home in Hoboken."

Frieda and Golda had formed a natural fundraising team. Frieda came to life in the presence of Golda as their messages of warning and hope intersected. A date was set for a meeting at Tessie's house.

I can't hide my excitement and turn to Teddy. "I feel like we just launched a movement," I said.

Teddy smiles, "I'm not sure we did all that much, Hannah. But I know we helped."

That evening, Teddy walks me home, and I ask him to come in for coffee. After the children go to bed, we have the apartment to ourselves. As we sit down, Teddy begins talking. His voice is shaky, and a sheen of perspiration appears on his forehead. He puts his hand in his pocket and takes out a letter in an envelope. "What's this?" I ask.

"I hope you'll read this *Help Me Hannah* letter and give it your attention and consideration. I think this one is really important."

"Sure, I will, Teddy," I answer, feeling somewhat confused. "Now?"

"Please read it now," Teddy says, his voice even more shaky.

I slowly open the envelope, not sure why this of all of the letters we receive is so important.

# Help Me Hannah # 4

*Dearest Hannah,*

*I am a middle-aged man who has never married. I have no family to support and I have thrown myself into my business. I assumed this would be the way of my whole life.*

*Recently, I met a lovely young widow with two children. When I am with her I feel more alive than I ever have in all my days. When I'm not with her, I think of her constantly. She is very beautiful, and I am very plain. I can't imagine a woman like this would want me in a physical way.*

*We have developed a friendship, but for me it's not enough. My problem is this: How can I move beyond friendship?*

*Signed,*

*A man in love*

With my heart pounding, I put the letter down. I take Teddy's hand in mine. I move closer to him and we kiss, at first gently, then with a passion that I've never known. The kiss goes on and neither one of us is able to break free. Then I slowly lead him into the bedroom. As I begin to remove my clothes Teddy starts to kiss me again, this time with intense desire. I find it hard to breathe. I guide him onto the bed, and our natural instincts take over. Teddy's hands explore my body, and I do the same with him. Our movements quicken.

After we both reach a climax, Teddy rolls over and we release one another. Teddy says, "Do you always respond to *Help Me Hannah* letters this way?" We both laugh, and before you know it, we kiss again… it seems we can't get enough of each other. Like two teenagers.

Teddy stays the night, but he leaves early in the morning, before the children wake up. My heart is full. Unexpected joys await me, I just know it. This wonderful man has come into my life. And I have no intention of ever letting him go.

# Part 3: More Letters

## Tessie's Idea

A week later, Tessie arrives. She's in my kitchen, coat off, looking more distressed than usual. As soon as I bring the pot of tea to the table, Tessie falls apart.

"Simon did it again. This time he's really in trouble. After only two weeks working at the factory, he gets into a fight with a co-worker, who according to Simon, is an anti-Semite. The man accused my Simon of trying to work faster than everyone else to get ahead. Calls him a *job killer*. The man said, loud enough for all to hear, "What do you expect from a Jew anyway?""

"This set Simon off, and he threw a punch. Of course, Simon is the one who got fired, throwing a punch like that. Now, again, he's out of work. I don't know how much longer I can take it Hannah."

I pause before responding to Tessie. She's right about Simon. He's a short, stocky man who doesn't seem to understand his own strength. He walks around with a chip on his shoulder, always ready for a fight. But under his bright blue eyes, there is turmoil and a need to be understood and respected. He gave up so much to move to *the goldena medina*. Marrying Tessie was a big step for him. She came from better stock than he did back in Hungary.

"You know Tessie, Simon doesn't seem to be a person who can work with other people. He's strong and a very hard worker. But that temper is the problem. Maybe he needs to find work where he doesn't interact with others. Start his own business."

Tessie nods her head slowly, pondering the implications. "If we could only point him in the right direction. I've been considering a few things for him. Like maybe a cleaning service during off-hours—for bars and restaurants after closing. I could even help him. When no one is around, Simon can be a talented man. He'll fix things if they break. He can polish the brass, touch up with paint. A bar that looks clean and shiny is attractive to customers. And lord knows, Hoboken has enough bars to keep him very busy."

I reply, "This sounds promising to me Tessie."

"From your mouth to God's ears, Hannah."

Tessie pauses for just a second, probably realizing that her troubles were monopolizing the conversation. "And how was your week, Hannah?"

"I thought you'd never ask…" I slowly look up from my cup and saucer with a sheepish grin. "I'm floating on cloud nine. We finally went to the next step, Teddy and me, if you know what I mean. And it feels wonderful. When he holds me in his arms, it's magic, Tessie. We've both been feeling something for one another for a long time now. He's a kind, gentle, intelligent, loving man. And we are VERY compatible, if you know what I mean." We both laugh, yes…. Tessie knows what I mean.

After Tessie leaves, I sit down with a cup of tea and read some of the letters that Teddy has given me - possible entries for my column. There are 25 letters to choose from for this week. I'm amazed at my little slice of success. I sure hope this keeps up. I want to be a part of Teddy's life. But it must stay professional too. He needs to respect me as a colleague, not just as a lover.

I chose this letter, so beautiful to me.

# Help Me Hannah # 5

*Dear Hannah,*

*My dear father died last month. He was a very special man. He had a wonderful relationship with my daughter, who I will call Rita. My father had become nearly blind towards the end of his life. He came to live with us so that we could help him, as he was a widower and all alone. He kept to himself and I sensed that he was quite depressed. He spent his time praying. My father was a very religious man.*

*When my daughter Rita was born, all that changed. It was as if he was young again. He had just enough sight left to help me take care of her. In time, my father learned how to change her diaper using his sense of touch. He was even able to feed her, with my help. He made wooden toys for her, and he built a beautiful dollhouse. His blindness wasn't a hindrance, amazingly.*

*As Rita got old enough, she became her grandfather's caretaker. She helped him cross the street and shop at the corner market. They were a real team. As my father grew older, he counted on Rita more and more.*

*Now that my father's gone, Rita is lost. Her grief is preventing her from moving forward.*

*Hannah, please help me heal my daughter's broken heart.*

*Signed,*

*Grieving in Brooklyn*

· · · · · · ·

*Dear Grieving in Brooklyn,*

*Your daughter's grief is normal. And only time will heal it. Let her say a prayer for her grandfather each day. Have her say Kaddish for him. These rituals are designed to help us deal with our grief.*

*I want you to think about all that Rita has learned. Her grandfather taught her about the meaning of love, kindness, and interdependence. Those lessons will remain for her whole life.*

# Tempers Flare

It's Saturday. My 'visit with Tessie' day. But I am traveling to Hoboken to see her this time, a reversal of our "usual." Tessie sounded distressed on the phone. "I'm not able to make the trip to Washington Heights today Hannah," she tells me.

I know that voice. I hear the distress. My turn to be supportive. Better not to tell her I'm coming. She'll say no, I'm sure.

"Mom…. ccccan I go with you on the fffferry? I want to go too. I can play with Alvin. He promised to show me some more magic tricks." I decide to bring Solly along. Franny wants to stay home and work on her hat design. She promises me she'll do her leg exercises.

When we arrive at 1235 Bloomfield Street and walk up the steps, I have a feeling of dread. I ring the bell and Simon answers. "What are you doing here Hannah? We don't need your help," he mutters and closes the door. I beg him to let me in, without success.

"Come on Solly, let's go," I take his hand.

Walking down the street, Solly spots Alvin playing ball against the stoop. We walk over together. Alvin has tears in his eyes.

"What's wrong honey?" I ask. This is not the Alvin I'm used to. He won't even look at me. "Is your Mom OK, Alvin?" I ask.

"No," says Alvin, with no explanation.

"Please take me to see her, Alvin. Can we go in through the back door? Your dad doesn't want me in the house. But I think your mom needs her friend today. What do you think, Alvin?"

"OK, Mrs. Altman. Maybe you can cheer her up. She hasn't gotten out of bed at all today. But I don't want Pop to be mad at me. Let's go through the door downstairs in the back. He won't see us."

With Alvin as my guide, we sneak in. He takes me to Tessie's bed, keeping the door closed. From the look on my friend's face, I'm sure something's wrong. I decide not to ask questions. We just sit together for a few minutes. I notice that she's holding her right arm above the elbow. Without being too obvious, I move her other arm away, and there's my answer. ...large red bruises.

Tessie finally speaks. "Simon's anger was against *me* this time Hannah. I suggested that he try the commercial cleaning business. I know he liked the idea, but he didn't like that it came from me. His pride was hurt, I guess. Then I got angry.

OK Hannah, you know me. I didn't choose my words so well.

Simon grabbed my arm and pulled, hard. I was knocked over and fell to the floor. He didn't hit me, but I could see he wanted to. He was holding himself back. To be honest Hannah, I was scared."

"I am too Tessie, for you. A man who hurts his wife....? Are you sure you're safe here?" Sometimes I wonder if Tessie brings on Simon's anger, on purpose or not.

"I know how to handle my husband, Hannah. After all these years, I can sense what will set him off. His insecurity is the very thing that makes him angry. When anyone questions his abilities, he loses his temper. Have you ever taken a good look at his hands? They're like the paws of a bear."

Tessie is right. She knows Simon only too well. But what to do? She has a family, two beautiful children who are the loves of her life. And no support other than Simon's meager and occasional earnings, plus the rent from her boarders.

Tessie reaches for my hand. "My head hurts again today, Hannah. I have been having awful headaches for weeks now. The fall to the floor didn't help. It helps to be in a dark room with a cold cloth on my forehead. Aspirin helps for a few hours, until the pain comes back."

"You need to come to the office and see my uncle. I know he can help with your headaches," I tell my friend with a squeeze to her hand. Tessie responds with a meek smile.

She's in pain. This is so unlike my Tessie. I'm worried, but I try not to show it. Right now, she needs a strong hand of friendship.

"Tessie, I have to leave now. But please let me make an appointment for you to see Uncle Ben."

"I need to think about it Hannah. Simon would be furious if anyone knew about him knocking me over. I just can't," Tessie says in a small, soft voice. I have to respect her feelings, but I won't let this go.

After our brief visit, I leave the house without Simon hearing me. I meet up with Solly. Alvin is in the middle of showing him a magic trick with a deck of cards. Solly is a perfect audience. He worships his friend Alvin. I grab Solly's hand, say a polite goodbye to Alvin, and head for the ferry. I try to act as if things are normal. The Lester children don't need to know what I've observed. It makes me worry for the children too. Does Simon lose his temper with them as well? I have never seen evidence of bruising on Alvin or Alice, thank goodness.

Back home, I sit down and review my Help Me Hannah Letters. Somehow, reading the letters empowers me, calms me down. I can't wait to begin. One letter fascinates me. I take out my pen and paper, close my eyes and imagine the character who is asking for my help. I see her as a beautiful, wild young woman.

# Help Me Hannah # 6

*Dear Hannah,*

*My story is one of success but also shame. I was born into a very religious family. My parents arranged a marriage for me to a very old man with a long beard. I was only sixteen at the time. He was repulsive and I refused to get into bed with him. The next morning, I ran away across the country and made my way to Washington State. I heard about gold being discovered in Alaska. Lots of people were traveling there from Washington to make their fortunes. Being desperate, I joined these brave souls in the hopes of making some money for myself.*

*Once I arrived I found work, and after some time I opened a tavern for prospectors. Men came to drink, gamble, play cards, and swap stories about gold. They paid their bills with gold nuggets and gold dust. Many loose women worked at my tavern. I had a good reputation, and I was proud that I ran an honest and clean establishment. There were so many lonely men that the women had lots of customers. I assisted in these sorts of transactions.*

*I made a good life for myself in Alaska, but now I want to come home to New York. I have sent my family money and gold nuggets to help them out during the hard times. I know they appreciate these gifts. But I'm worried that they will judge me harshly.*

*My question is: Will my family accept me, knowing that my life has been so very different from theirs? I no longer follow the rules of kashrut. I don't observe Shabbos. My relationships have not been the usual. I have friends of all types, and all religions. I've had many boyfriends. I'm surely not a good little Shayne Maydele that they remember.*

*Sincerely,*

*Annie, a homesick woman*

· · · · · · ·

*Dear Annie,*

*There will be some who will judge you. There will be some who accept you. There will be some who admire you. You are obviously very strong. And you probably have the resources to start a very comfortable new life in New York City.*

*If your family questions you, be careful with your answers. They only need to know as much as you feel comfortable telling them. They will be happier if you tell them only what they want to hear. Let their imaginations fill in the blanks.*

*Good luck to you.*

*Hannah*

# Headaches Always Headaches

After a long day at work, I find myself walking home, slowly, and thinking about my best friend. If Tessie's problem was a *Help Me Hannah* letter, what would I advise? Simon has a temper, we always knew that. But to be so angry that you knock your wife to the ground? That's not normal. And Tessie's headaches - it's no wonder. She's under all that stress. A good friend needs to listen, to advise, to help. That's my dilemma. I think at this point I should listen, and wait. Sometimes words can get you in trouble. It takes skill to be a good listener. I pride myself on that. Next Saturday, when Tessie comes to visit, the right words will come to me.

Franny and Solly are sitting at the kitchen table doing homework when I arrive home. Solly is busy practicing his nine times tables, aloud, with Franny as his coach. He's doing a fine job, no stuttering today. I think memorization is good for his speech problem. Maybe he should branch out into reciting poems too," I say to myself. Anyway...proud Mama is beaming. Lucky me to have such great children. I'm quietly *qvelling*.

Suppertime, and what shall we have? Franny hasn't taken to cooking as I had hoped, and I can't blame her. She has enough on her plate, so I decided not to add any more pressure. She has to continue her leg exercises, along with

105

caring for her little brother. Although she has fully recovered from polio, there is some leftover weakness, Uncle Ben tells me. We can't let up on her routine. How much responsibility can I put on my daughter?

I decide to make a light dairy meal for us. I'll open a can of salmon, put out bananas and sour cream (my favorite), and some cucumber salad that I made on Sunday. As I'm preparing, the children are finishing up their work.

The doorbell rings and I find Teddy standing there with a big grin on his face. As he walks in, he can't wait to tell me…. "Well Miss Advice Columnist, your last *Help Me Hannah* letter was a big hit. It created a lot of conversation among our staff. We called your homesick letter writer Klondike Annie. Everyone had an opinion about her.

"And we got over one hundred letters with comments and opinions. Plus…. we received more *Help Me Hannah* letters than ever before. I wanted to bring them to you tonight so that you can begin choosing the next one," Teddy says while handing me a thick brown envelope.

As I listened to Teddy, a wave of excitement washed over me. Pride in my work, and that same warm, glowing feeling I get when I stand next to Teddy. He draws me to him and gives me quick hug.

"I can't believe it Teddy," I reply. "Well, maybe I can. I knew it was a great story and I felt that people could relate to her problem. We all want to be accepted, and our little, tavern owner is no different."

Teddy continued, "The success of your column will give my ad salesmen a great way to get more revenue for the paper. Circulation is up and that's always the bottom line.

"Teddy, I just put dinner on the table. It's not much, but we would love you to sit down and eat supper with us. The kids will be happy, and so will I," I say and feel myself blushing at the same time.

The evening feels natural and right. Teddy sees Solly's work, and asks him to recite the 9 times table. He's happy to oblige, although he stutters briefly. Franny shows Teddy the hat design she's been working on. Teddy says, "Franny, keep it up. Maybe we can advertise in *The Jewish Gazette* for you. I can see it now, *Custom Hats by Frances Altman.*" Franny laughs and makes a face. "Maybe someday when I'm a lot older," she says.

I know she feels proud. Teddy has a way of making people feel good about themselves. That I know from personal experience.

After supper Teddy gives me a hand clearing the table. Tonight he doesn't stay too long, sensing that the kids need me. I'm a little disappointed, but glad that he made a special visit with the *Help Me Hannah* letters. *After all, we are professional colleagues,* I think to myself, *sort of ....*

When Saturday arrives, Tessie comes over for her usual visit. Her arm is healed now, and she tells me she wanted to get out of the house today, away from Simon. Alvin comes along too, with his new yo-yo to show Solly. Tessie's daughter Alice is staying at home with Simon. Tessie feels that Alice will keep him calm. He adores his daughter. Everyone does. She's a charming teenage girl, the pride and joy of the Lester family. If Alice encourages Simon to pursue the cleaning business, he might go along with the idea.

"Things are looking up, Hannah," says Tessie as she slowly sips her tea with sugar and munches on a piece of mandel bread. "Simon seems to feel some shame for what he did last week. He's been quite loving to me these days. And I was able to set up two cleaning jobs for him. But I was very careful with my words. He didn't get mad this time, Hannah. If he keeps his temper in check, these two jobs will be a great start. One is a clothing shop around the corner, and the other is a small tavern. He can work in the evening at the clothing store, and then early morning at the tavern."

I'm glad I was a good listener this time. Better not to give advice to Tessie. I'm hopeful the storm has passed for my dear friend. After our visit, Tessie gets up to leave. The scent of Evening in Paris is leaving my kitchen along with Tessie.

"I better head home, Hannah. I can feel a headache starting again." But before she puts on her coat, she asks me about Teddy.

"Let's just say all is well. I don't want to give myself a *kinehora.*"

Tessie gives me a poke, laughs, and goes off to find Alvin and start her trip home on the ferry.

# Recipe for Cucumber Salad

This one is easy. Make this on a hot summer day, as a perfect side dish for a light supper. I like it with sour cream, but it's fine without.

**Thinly slice cucumber**
**Add:**
¼ t salt
¼ t sugar
¼ t vinegar (wine vinegar or regular)
**Let sit, then drain water**

**Add to taste:**
**Dill, parsley, and sour cream (optional)**

Keep cold. The amounts are for 1 cucumber. Increase by ¼ t for each additional cucumber.

# Opportunity Knocks

I start at work on Thursday by checking the appointment book before Uncle Ben arrives at the office. Teddy will be our last appointment again. His scoliosis treatments are giving him relief from his pain. I wonder if he continues to come in weekly just because of me. I hope so.

When 4:00 rolls around, I check my face in my compact mirror and give my hair a little combing, tucking my page boy curl under, powdering my nose. I know Uncle Ben notices because of that little smirk on his face. He's so fond of Teddy. A good romance makes everyone feel good.

Teddy and I go to our favorite—Goldberg's delicatessen around the corner. We order our pastrami sandwich with a cream soda to share, and some apple strudel for dessert. Teddy tells me that Golda Meir has contacted him from her travels across the country. Her fundraising events for the Pioneer Women Organization are going very well. She's recruiting Jewish people to return to the homeland and help the cause. They need bodies to farm the land, and create settlements for needy Jews from countries where there is persecution. She has asked for another article in *The Jewish Gazette*.

"I want to interview her and do a feature story with photographs to create interest. Will you come along and help me with the interview, Hannah? I know Golda likes you."

"I would love to be with you for the interview, Teddy. I admire Golda. Do you think I can bring Franny? She talks about Golda all the time. What a wonderful role model for my daughter."

"That would be fine Hannah," says Teddy as he walks me home. We're holding hands and anticipating things to come.

"Please come in tonight, Teddy. We can take this time to think of questions for the interview." That's me, always the professional.

Teddy smiles at me and says, "Why not?" As we walk into the kitchen, Solly runs up to Teddy and shows him a magic trick that Alvin taught him—"The four bank robbers in a deck of cards."

"And I have a trick to show you Solly," as Teddy pulls a magical quarter from behind Solly's ear. Franny says a polite hello and goes off to the bedroom to read. She thinks these magic tricks are so corny.

Teddy and I snuggle on the sofa in the front parlor. It seems we can be together for hours. We make our plan. Teddy puts his arm around me in a familiar, comfortable way. Once the children are safely asleep in their beds, he reaches over and pulls me close. My body responds with a hunger that almost embarrasses me. Teddy's lips meet mine and we confirm our love once again, this time with more passion than ever before. He spends the night, but leaves early again, before the children wake up.

On Saturday morning, Franny asks me if she can bring her hat designs to the office to show Golda. "Mom," she says, "When Golda gives her speeches at synagogues and homes of wealthy Jewish donors, she needs to look the part. My hats will give her prestige, at least I think so," she laughs.

"I'm glad you're so modest," I tease. "Sure, my dear daughter, bring one or two hats." We gather our things and head to the subway. Solly is at our neighbor Claire's apartment for the day. She's been wonderful at helping me out. I remind myself to bake a batch of mandel bread for her.

Golda and Teddy stand up when we arrive. We all embrace. Golda remembers Franny from the first fundraiser at Uncle Ben and Aunt Rose's home. After some small talk, Golda begins.

"I want the Jews of the United States to become as passionate as I am about our homeland. We need to plant trees, build hospitals, create farms, build irrigation tunnels. Sadly, we'll need weapons too. We're surrounded by enemies. It's about time that we have a safe haven for oppressed Jews. Europe is a perfect example. We all have family in the old country. Will the United States take them in? History has shown us that the answer is no."

Golda gives us lots of material for an important piece for the newspaper. We're all satisfied with our alliance. "I love your hat, Franny," Golda says.

Franny replies, "I brought two for you Mrs. Meir. When I was at home healing from polio, I began designing these hats. Mom got me started. I made you this blue hat because you will look striking and stylish with this hat on."

Golda was impressed. "I admire your work and your maturity, Franny. Your confidence shows me that you have great potential. I want you to consider joining me in my cause. We have a kibbutz that could use a special young lady like you to work with children. You could work on teaching English. Maybe you could learn a thing or two about farming."

Franny lights up.... "I want to go with you Mrs. Meir. Mom, please let me."

"We need to talk about this first, Franny. I'm not sure that you're strong enough to travel. And I'm not sure if I'm strong enough to let you go," I tell my daughter.

Although I have to admit I was mildly irritated by Golda's presumptuousness with Franny, I was also awed by the fervor with which she is trying to build a country that would support and protect Jews from around the world.

"Golda, let's stay in touch," I said with a smile. "You have been an inspiration to Franny and me. I wish we could take you up on your offer. But this isn't the right time."

Golda nodded. "Maybe when you're older, Franny. We also need help right here in New York. We need to fill those blue boxes with coins for planting trees."

"I've got still more people to see and places to go," said Golda as she popped her new hat on her head and waved goodbye.

As soon as I get home, I remember that I promised Teddy a new *Help Me Hannah* Letter. I found a perfect addition. Hmmm, let me decide how to advise this loving father.

# Help Me Hannah # 7

*Please Help Me Hannah,*

*I am a father with a wonderful family. God has given me a good wife and four beautiful children. But there is a problem. I am deaf and so is my wife. All four of my children are hearing. I became deaf after having measles as a young child. My wife suffered from a severe ear infection as a child and also lost her hearing.*

*Our children help us when we go shopping and when we have to deal with others in our neighborhood. Luckily, I have a good job in a machine shop working with my hands.*

*We keep a kosher home and follow the laws of Shabbos. My oldest son will be of Bar Mitzvah age very soon. Judaism means a lot to us. I want to be able to "hear" his haftorah. I wish there would be a Shul that would use sign language.*

*Hannah, would you please ask your dear readers if there is any hope for my request?*

*With respect,*

*A devoted father*

· · · · · · ·

*Dear Devoted Father,*

*I am asking the many readers of The Jewish Gazette if anyone can help this good man. Perhaps there is someone who is fluent in Hebrew and sign language who can "translate" the Torah portion for this family.*

*There is a need for our community to include deaf people in our rituals. I'm sure there are many families who would benefit from a service in sign language. The Jewish Federation must address this important concern.*

*We at The Jewish Gazette welcome correspondence from any readers who might be of help. We will be in touch with you if we get a response.*

# Part 4: One Year Later

## Daughter Drama

"He's perfect for her. Why won't Alice listen to me?" Tessie announces as she storms through the door.

It's Saturday, and of course my best friend is here for our weekly visit. I rely on these talks lately, more than ever. Here we are, a year later, still talking about our lives, problems, and joys. Some things never change. Tessie is still running Alice's life. And still complaining that no one listens to her. Although today she says she feels pretty well, even though her headaches have been more frequent than ever.

But there is some good news too. Simon's cleaning business is doing well. The Lester family has food on the table. I think the situation works because Simon doesn't interact with people while cleaning during off hours. He works like a bull, gets his jobs done. No fights, no accusations of antisemitism. Tessie handles the payments. Alice and Tessie are the ones who interact with the clients on behalf of Simon.

But….my Tessie is never satisfied. She thrives on drama. This week, the drama is about Alice and her boyfriend.

"Why not let Alice choose?" I say.

"My Alice, with her beauty and her brains will not waste her life with a delivery boy, not if I have anything to do with it. She met a man last week who has shown interest in her. Ok, so he's ten years older than Alice. He's kind of bald too, with a little belly. But Jake comes from a wealthy family. He drives a Cadillac. He's asked her out, Hannah. Alice doesn't want to see him again, no interest. I insist that she give him a chance. Maybe it will be *beshert.*"

*"Beshert* with your intervention? Not sure that's the way it works."

Tessie gives me a look and says, "We'll see about that. And Hannah, how is your Frances doing? When I see her these days, there's barely a limp. I think you caught the polio early enough to have a good recovery. And she told me about the opportunity to go to Palestine. Golda has made quite an impact on your daughter."

"Well, that is *my* 'daughter drama' dear Tessie. Golda tells me she has a plan for Franny. That I shouldn't worry. She knows of an organization called Youth Aliyah. They've begun to set up a kibbutz for young people fleeing Nazi Germany. With Franny's talents and intelligence, she can be an inspiration to the children when they arrive in the homeland. Franny reminds me that her papa called her a little teacher and little mother for Solly, so why can't she do that with immigrant children in Palestine? How can I get in the way of her passion, her dream, her opportunity? But I worry. Is it safe? And she's so young."

I feel better after I verbalize my fears. They don't sound so bad when I talk about them as they sound inside my head.

Tessie thinks a moment and says, "Hannah, what would you do if someone asked you that very same question in a *Help Me Hannah* letter? What would your answer be? Your advice is always wise. Have trust in yourself. And have trust in your own daughter."

"That's what Teddy keeps telling me. My two confidants agree. What more proof do I need?" I answer.

Just then Frances walks into the kitchen and gives Tessie a big hug. I suspect she's been listening to our conversation, but I decide to ignore that fact. Franny is on her way to her youth group meeting.

We say our goodbyes and just as I start cleaning up, there's a knock on my door. It's Uncle Ben. He asks to come in because he needs to discuss something important. I'm curious. Work is going very well. The patients are used to me now, the front desk is organized. What could be the problem? I hope Aunt Rose and little Michael are well. Rose has become a better mother, high strung, but very loving.

"Come and sit down, Uncle Ben. Would you like a glass of tea?" My uncle has a pained look on his face that he's trying to hide. My heart sinks.

# One Door Closes, Another One Opens

I study his expression. "Whatever you must tell me dear Uncle, don't worry. I can handle it." I bring him his tea in a glass with a sugar cube. He takes a sip.

With his head bent, his eyes look up into mine. "Oy Hannah, your Aunt Rose has decided to come back to work. She's hired a competent babysitter for Michael. She misses work terribly. But you know what that means?"

My heart sinks. I try to keep my emotions inside. "I understand, and please don't feel responsible for me. My income at the office has taken me through a rough period in my life. Now I have job experience. The children are used to me working. I'll find another job, Uncle."

"Let's have the two of you work together next week for a smooth transition. During that time, you will be able to search the want ads for a suitable position. You know I will give you a fine letter of recommendation, Hannah," my uncle says.

"Thank you for believing in me," I say to Uncle Ben as we walk to the front door. We embrace, and I watch him walk slowly down the sidewalk. My Uncle's a sensitive man, like most of our family. This is difficult for him. Rose is the strong one in their marriage. I'm sure she'll be glad when I leave the office.

After he leaves, I sink into my chair and wonder, "What am I going to do now?"

On Monday when I walk into the office, Aunt Rose is at her desk looking very important. "Good morning, Hannah. It feels good to be back. I thank you for helping us out. Now if you'll excuse me, I need to set up for the first patient."

I smile curtly, and try to look busy at the front desk. "Time to move on," I tell myself. I can't wait to meet Teddy after work at Goldberg's. I can already picture us at the table, talking and eating that potato knish. And I know Teddy will comfort me. I need that today. The thought of Teddy's welcoming arms gives me a sense of security that I've never known before, even when I was married to Abe. Teddy is compassionate. He always has the right words for me.

As the day goes on, I find myself disconnecting. Aunt Rose is in her glory. The patients are happy to see her again, and why not? I feel like a fifth wheel now. I look at my watch, which moves at a snail's pace. When 5:00 arrives, I take my coat, say goodbye, and almost run out to the sidewalk. I'll be with Teddy before I know it.

As I walk through the door of Goldberg's Delicatessen, I spot Teddy right away. "Come sit down Hannah. I was able to get our favorite table. I took the liberty of ordering our usual," Teddy tells me as I fall into the chair. "Hannah, what's wrong? You look as if you've seen a ghost."

I begin to tell him about losing my job, and tears well up in my eyes. Teddy immediately soothes me with his touch. Now I'm sobbing. I needed to express my sorrow in a safe place. Teddy has become my safe place.

"Hannah, please listen to me. I've been pondering this plan for a while. The timing couldn't be better. *The Jewish Gazette's* circulation is steadily increasing. Our ad sales have been improving too. Your advice column is extremely popular. It's time for you to be on our payroll. You can work on *Help Me Hannah* more diligently now. And I can use an assistant to help me with day-to-day tasks. Your help would free me up to concentrate on the business side of the paper."

"Did God put you on this earth to save my life Teddy? It sure feels that way," I tell him. "It may sound overly dramatic but that's the way I feel sometimes."

"I'm not sure if God has enough free time to worry about you and me Hannah. But sometimes I feel as if our meeting was magic. Maybe it was just the right timing for both of us. Please think about my offer Hannah. I really need help. And soon." Teddy's words are coming at me so fast I'm having trouble breathing.

In my mind I am thrilled with the idea of working at *The Jewish Gazette* with Teddy. I hope it won't put a strain on our relationship. I'll gladly take the risk.

We begin to talk about other things, and I say, "Teddy, remember when Solly acted in the play at Camp Garden of Eden? Well, he has been wanting to act again. I don't want to stand in his way. The Jewish Community Center is going to put on a play. One of the members wrote a play based on a Sholem Aleichem story, called *Tevye, the Dairyman.* Solly tried out and was accepted to play the part of one of the boys in the village. He has a few lines. And Franny, always the supportive sister, will be helping with the costumes again. I'm glad they'll be working together. The best part is that he never stutters on stage."

"Hannah, that will be good for him. You worry about Solly's stutter, but I think he'll outgrow it. Most kids do." Teddy knows just what to say.

"Let's get you home, Hannah. I need a new advice letter for next week. Help Me Hannah," Teddy says in his most dramatic voice, hands in prayer position. I give Teddy a little poke and he pulls me close and kisses the top of my head.

At home at my kitchen table, I get right to work. Teddy has given me thirty letters this time. I have to find the right one. I love this work. So many people have hidden problems in their lives, and it's good to know I can help. I look through them all and decide to use this one.

# Help Me Hannah # 8

Dear Hannah,

*My husband Carl (I've changed his name for privacy) is a barber in our small city in New Jersey. He is a wonderful man who is loved by all. He is very intelligent, with many operations going on inside his place of business. Officially, it's The Carteret Barber Shop. But Carl also sells insurance, does tooth extractions, writes letters for his illiterate customers. He even does cupping and leeching. He's the president of our synagogue. Everyone thinks of my husband as a scholar. He speaks seven languages. Not many people know he only has a fifth-grade education.*

*Carl has a love of modern machines and gadgets too. We have a radio, a victrola with a big horn, a Frigidaire, and of course his pride and joy - a big beautiful Buick Roadster.*

*Why am I writing to you? I should be happy, proud of my husband.*

*But Carl has a secret. He's not as rich as everyone thinks. Carl is a big spender. He never checks the prices of the things that he desires. He loves to play the numbers, and cards with his buddies. If people knew about our financial troubles, Carl would be ashamed and so would I. His reputation would sink, I'm sure.*

*Please help me Hannah. I don't know what to do.*

*Respectfully,*

*A concerned wife*

· · · · · · ·

*Dear Concerned Wife,*

*Your husband sounds like a man who lives life to the fullest. Men like Carl often ignore everyday practical things like paying bills and being frugal. He loves excitement which is why he gambles. These qualities make him fun to be with, both for you and members of your community.*

*He will bring you down with him if he doesn't get his spending under control. If you are willing to take this chance, then do nothing. But you can be the master of your own fate. Tell Carl that you must hold the purse strings in your household from now on. You keep the budget. You keep the ledger for his business. You keep the money. Give him only what he needs for spending. If, after 6 months, the bank account stays stabile, you will have made a life-saving change. If Carl can't stop his irresponsible ways, you may have to threaten him with exposure.*

*I believe that your husband would be ashamed if his clients and friends knew of his financial woes. Hopefully the threat of humiliation will be just the tactic you need.*

# New Job, New Challenge

This is my third day working in the office of *The Jewish Gazette*. Teddy has told me so much about this place that I already feel comfortable. Being the only woman in the office feels a little strange, but I'll get used to it.

Teddy, being the kind of man that he is, has introduced me to the staff in the most welcoming and professional way. They all know about my *Help Me Hannah* column. "It feels good to be a part of this team," I tell myself.

My desk is right next to Teddy's, as I am his assistant as well as the writer for my very own advice column. All the desks are close together, and the constant tapping of typewriters provides gentle background music. I give a quick thought about Solly and Franny, hoping that they're happy in school today. Solly seemed a little teary this morning, but I can't let that throw me off. "Once a mother - always a mother," I say to myself with a sigh.

I'm wearing my dark green pleated skirt and cream-colored sweater, my pearls, heels and silk stockings, of course. I noticed a look of approval on Teddy's face as I walked in at 9:00 AM sharp. I take a cup of coffee and sit down at my desk.

"Let's work on office matters today. I would like you to take over some of my duties," Teddy says and he hands me a huge stack of papers and folders. "I need some kind of organization here. I have no time to file things, so they sit on my desk and pile up."

We work together and slowly I begin to see a method for organizing Teddy's very messy desk. "Let me work on creating a better filing system, Teddy. If it's okay with you, I'll get this project started this morning, and then work on my *Help Me Hannah* letters after lunch. If you are able to find things easily, it will save you time."

"If you can accomplish that Hannah, I will be forever grateful. Time is what I need these days," Teddy responds. I can see the look of relief on his face.

By reading through the files and with Teddy's guidance, I'm slowly learning the way things work around here. I'm humbled by the amount of work that goes into publishing a daily newspaper. Advertising, circulation, editorials, classifieds, page layout, dealing with the printers—so much to learn.

It's lunchtime and Teddy asks me to join him at the Main Line Diner across the street. The diner is a converted railroad car. While we wait for the waitress to bring my tuna sandwich and Teddy's grilled cheese, we sip some tea and gaze longingly at the cakes under glass on the counter.

Teddy looks at me and seems a little nervous. "What's wrong Teddy?" I ask.

"I think it's time for you to meet my family," he says, looking down and fiddling with the silverware on the table in front of him. "I've told my mother and sisters about you. They're not used to me having a 'lady friend', as they like to say. I would like to invite you to come for a visit this Sunday afternoon."

"I would love to, Teddy," I say with a smile, trying to sound enthusiastic. Deep down I'm not so sure. After all, I'm a widow with two children. Teddy has never been married. These women are used to having him all to themselves. "Should I bring Frances and Solly?"

"Maybe for our first introduction you should come alone Hannah. It's a lot for them to take in," Teddy says softly.

His tone worries me. I know that Teddy has been the sole support of these ladies for some time now, ever since his father died. They rely on Teddy for everything. He's their emotional rock.

"Whatever you think is best," I say with a tentative smile. I hate to leave the children on a Sunday. But I have faith in Teddy's advice. He will know what's best when it comes to his own mother.

Back at the office, I get started on the *Help Me Hannah* letter. Looking through the stack, I find one about music and love.

I think this one will be interesting to my readers. This young girl really needs some guidance.

# Help Me Hannah # 9

Dear Hannah,

*All of my life I have been a good girl. I am the only child to parents from Warsaw. They want me to have a better life in the new world. We all love to listen to classical music every night as we tune in to WQXR on our radio.*

*But my love for music is part of my problem. I'm fourteen years old. I have been taking piano lessons for five years now. My parents have saved every penny so that I can continue. I practice my scales and classical pieces for two hours a day. Mr. M is my wonderful music teacher, my friend, my everything.*

*I am in love with him, and I know he loves me too. I walk to his house every Tuesday, after school at 4:00. Last week, during the lesson he tried to kiss me and I let him. It was thrilling for me. I think about that kiss every minute of every day.*

*My dear teacher understands me. We both have a passion for Bach and Beethoven. Sometimes he sits right next to me and we play duets. Mr. M recognizes my love for music. He tells me that I have talent.*

*Mr. M is a married man and he is twenty years older than me. People would say that I am very young and maybe don't understand true love. But I do love him. Yet, I know in my heart that if I continue to allow him to kiss me, it would be wrong.*

*Now I don't know what to do. I want Mr. M to kiss me again. If my parents find out, I'm worried they will stop my music lessons. I don't want to stop so I'm afraid to tell them.*

*Please Hannah, help me decide what to do. I am very confused.*

*Yours truly,*

*Pauline*

· · · · · · ·

*Dear Pauline,*

*You have an obligation to tell your parents about the kiss. You are too young to handle this problem alone. Mr. M is a married man. If you continue, you may break up a family. To Mr. M, you are a young girl. Piano lessons have brought you close together. But your age difference is too great. This is a dangerous situation for you.*

*Your parents will probably get a different teacher for you. But for now, the relationship will only bring trouble and disappointment.*

# Family Matters

I can't wait for Tessie to arrive. I need to tell her about the visit with Teddy's family. I baked a double batch of sponge cake. I brought half to Teddy's apartment and saved the rest for us at home. My kids love that cake.

I put a few slices on my fancy plate and boil the water for tea. As the door opens after a quick knock, the scent of Evening in Paris arrives with my best friend following, not far behind.

As soon as we sit down, Tessie says "Hannah, tell me about the visit with Teddy's mother and sisters. What are they like?"

"The visit went pretty well, I guess. The sisters were fine. But Teddy's mother, Mrs. Damsky, was cold to me. She thanked me for the sponge cake but said it wasn't necessary, and that her sponge cake is much lighter. She asked about my children but never asked to meet them. She asked too many questions. A nosy *yenta,* I would call her. She wanted to know why I have to work. How can I leave my children? How did my husband die, how long ago? It's pretty easy to see that she is suspicious. And maybe a little protective and possessive of Teddy.

"But at the end of my visit, I thanked them all and invited them to my house for Shabbos to meet Franny and Solly. The sisters were delighted. Teddy gave me an approving smile. Mrs. Damsky didn't respond."

Tessie thought for a moment and said, "Well, I think she sounds like trouble if you ask me. What kind of woman doesn't want her son to be happy? He finally falls in love with a lovely person like you, Hannah. A good mother would be happy about that."

Tessie changes the subject. I'm glad because I don't like to think anything can stand in the way of Teddy and me.

Tessie continues, "Alice told me that her boyfriend Joe wants to help Simon with his cleaning business. He's offered to drive him back and forth in the delivery truck. Simon has been walking and taking buses. It would be a big help. Oh, the boy is growing on me Hannah. But a future? I don't see it. That successful young man, Jake, has been after Alice but she doesn't want a second date. And you ask me why I have headaches? Oy, my life, always something to give me trouble. Why don't they ever listen to me?" she says, holding her head in her hands.

I try to think of the right way to approach this problem with Tessie. I decide, again, to listen and nod. I wish she would forget about this man, Jake. She wastes a lot of time and energy on directing the lives of her children and husband.

Sometimes I wonder about my own mothering style. I want my kids to do what makes them happy. For example, Franny's dream to work on a kibbutz when she's old enough. Solly and his theatre.…...Both can be dangerous in their own ways. Yet, I don't want to let my worries affect their plans. I think my kids are pretty independent, and I'm happy about that.

Tessie looks a little pale. "Are you ok?" I ask. "I don't like the color of your face right now."

"I have a headache again. I felt it coming on this morning, but I didn't want to miss our visit. I better go home now Hannah. Sorry. I need to lie down. I think I better make an appointment with your Uncle Ben about my problem. Maybe he can help me," she says while walking out the door. I walk with her to the subway to make sure that she can make it. She seems strong enough. We embrace as we say goodbye.

# Recipe for Sponge Cake

I've been talking about sponge cake and I'd like to share my family's recipe with you, dear reader. To me, sponge cake isn't like fancy bakery cakes, it's simple and plain, no fancy frosting, no layers, just simple. That's not a bad thing ... simple is good.

**5 large eggs**

**¾ cup sugar**

**1 cup flour**

**Preheat oven to 350 degrees**

**Beat 5 eggs with sugar until the mixture is very high and fluffy**

**Fold in flour a little bit at a time. Do not overmix or you will lose fluffiness.**

**Add batter into a 9x12 pan or a round springform pan**

Bake at 350 degrees for 30 minutes. Check with wooden toothpick. It should come up clean.

# More Sponge Cake

"Mom, do you think I should wear the blue dress tonight?" Franny asks. We're preparing for our company and the Shabbos dinner.

"Yes, and Solly please wear your new white shirt. Franny, help me set the table. I want to check on my fricassee in the kitchen."

Once everything is ready, we sit and wait. I must admit, I'm a little nervous. My white lace tablecloth, candles on the table, challah under the embroidered cover, wine for kiddush ready to be poured. I will be serving a full dinner tonight, gefilte fish, matzoh ball soup, chicken fricassee, and fruit compote for dessert. Ah... wonderful smells are coming from the kitchen.

At six o'clock, the bell rings. Teddy arrives with the sisters, Mildred and Evelyn, and his mother trailing behind. Mrs. Damsky is carrying a covered plate.

"Thank you, Mrs. Damsky," I say as I take it from her hands. "Oh, it's a sponge cake. What a treat. It will go perfectly with my fruit compote," I say with a smile.

"Yes, Hannah, I want you to taste mine so you can see how light and fluffy a sponge cake can be. Maybe I'll show you the way I beat my egg whites. That's my little secret," she tells me.

And so, the evening begins. My kids make a good impression, although Solly is stuttering while he shows them the four robbers card trick. Franny saves the day by showing the ladies her hat designs. I can tell that Teddy's sisters are impressed. They seem genuinely interested in the children, and my kids respond warmly, showing them around the apartment proudly. Even Teddy's mother seems to soften, just a little, especially when we all rave about her light and fluffy sponge cake. By the time dinner is over, not a crumb is left on the plate.

Right before leaving, as the children are getting our guests their coats, Teddy pulls me aside. "You are amazing Hannah," he says and gives me a warm and very long kiss. I can see that I made him proud tonight. I feel a glow that I wish would last forever.

I think about how lucky I am to be working with Teddy at *The Jewish Gazette*. The latest *Help Me Hannah* letter reminds me of the importance of my work. I am honored to be doing this fine job of mine.

# Help Me Hannah # 10

*Dear Hannah,*

*I have a problem and it's preventing me from being truly happy.*

*You see, I am a young woman. My whole family was killed during a pogrom in my little shtetel in Russia. Bad things happened to me too. Now I have no one left. A kind uncle in New York brought me to this country and let me live with his family. He got me a job working in a laundry, ironing clothes for other people. Even though I'm grateful to be here, I am still very lonely.*

*A few months ago, I met a nice man. He is a bus driver, and makes a good living. He loves me and I love him. I finally feel happy, at last. He asked me to marry him. I said yes, but something is holding me back. What if he knew I was raped? He thinks I'm pure, but I'm not. If I tell him, he may decide to leave me. If I keep the secret, I will feel guilty.*

*Hurting,*

*Rachel from Russia*

• • • • • • •

*Dear Rachel,*

*Your story is not uncommon. Many young girls were raped during the pogroms. You are very strong because you started a new life for yourself in a new country. You are working and earning your keep.*

*You must tell your boyfriend about the rape. If he really loves you, he will understand. You deserve to have true love, without secrets.*

# Hospital

The phone rings early the next morning. It's Simon. "Tessie's at St. Mary's Hospital, Hannah, and she's asking for you," he tells me, with fear in his voice. "She fell last night, and we couldn't wake her. Alvin found her lying on the kitchen floor."

Trying to sound calm, I tell Simon that I'll be there soon. "I think my Uncle Ben should come too. He can help us understand what's going on. I've been telling Tessie to come to his office, but she never listens to me." It's the wrong time for scolding, I know. But I can't help it.

Uncle Ben tells me he'll pick me up after his house calls. Together we drive to Hoboken. As we enter Tessie's hospital room, I see Simon sitting by the bed holding Tessie's hand. This big strong man is frightened.

Tessie is sleeping. I stand next to Simon and put my arm around his shoulders. He barely reacts. Uncle Ben arranges to meet with the doctor who treated Tessie.

When my uncle comes back into the room his face looks pale. He tells Simon that Dr. Roche would like to speak to him. "Will you come with me please, Doc?" Simon pleads.

"I'm not so good at understanding medical words. Hannah, can you stay with Tessie? I don't want her to be alone if she wakes up."

Tessie is sleeping peacefully but after fifteen minutes, she wakes up, startled. "Why are you here, Hannah?" My strong, controlling friend isn't in control right now. "I don't understand what's going on."

I decide honesty is best. "You know that you fell yesterday. Alvin found you on the floor in the kitchen. The doctor has been observing you and did some tests. Simon is with the doctor now. Uncle Ben is with them too. You see, Tessie, your whole fan club is here," I say, trying to sound positive. I'm pretty scared though. Tessie's like a sister to me.

I'm no longer a Pollyanna after seeing my very own husband, Abe, pass away. I used to think life was fair and that God rewards good people and punishes the bad ones. Now I know better. Maybe these things are just luck, random, and that thought makes me uneasy. If something bad should happen to Tessie ... oh, I can't even think about that right now.

Just then, Simon and Uncle Ben come back into the room. Uncle Ben says, "Tessie, the doctors here at St. Mary's are concerned about your headaches and your 'spell' yesterday. Your heart and blood pressure are fine. Perhaps it's just nerves. But we must check further, in my opinion. It's safe for you to go home now. You must spend a week of bed rest."

Simon chimes in, "You see Tessie, I told you that you have to rest more. Stop working so hard. Let me and the kids take care of the boarders. I'm the man of the house, for God's sake. Leave it all to me."

Tessie, in her usual style, replies, "You? I should leave it all to you? Ha! Where would we be now if I left it up to you?" Simon hangs his head.

On the way home, I ask my uncle what he thinks could possibly be wrong with my friend. He tells me, "It's too soon to make a diagnosis, Hannah. I want to consult with my colleagues first. These cases take time. Right now, you can be helpful by being a good friend. Bring food to the house, watch the children, bring flowers. She'll need some cheering up next week. Bed rest is not Tessie's usual lifestyle, I assume."

"Bed rest? Tessie? From your mouth to God's ears." I groan.

# A Doctor's Help

The staff at *The Jewish Gazette* is buzzing about current affairs. Journalists have so much material these days. It's 1934, and FDR has done a fine job with his WPA projects: new roads, bridges, dams being built. The Dust Bowl is a big problem in the southwest. Unemployment is twenty two percent now, which is a big improvement, although there are still too many people out of work. President Roosevelt is very popular, so admired, that Simon Lester put a framed picture of him in their parlor.

The news from Europe is worrying all of us. Hitler was declared the Fuhrer. Stalin and Mao Tse Tung have been gaining power by spreading their communist doctrine.

We are living in a time when newspapers and radio are thriving. People are starved for knowledge of the world, and we at *The Jewish Gazette* are here to provide it. Teddy is pleased with our success, and he hints that I'm a big part of it. I don't mind the compliment, even though I doubt that it's true.

"I have an announcement," Teddy begins at our Friday morning staff meeting." WOR has reached out to me. They want to do an interview with our advice columnist."

Everyone looks at me with surprise. I can feel my face slowly turn red. I feel a little embarrassed but very excited about the prospect of being on the radio.

"Teddy, I can't believe it," I say when we sit down and get back to work. "I'm not ready for this. What will I say?"

"I'll be there with you, Hannah. We'll plan it all out. Be prepared with some of your most interesting letters and answers. We can practice beforehand," Teddy says, trying to give me confidence.

"Well, it will have to wait until after tomorrow. I want to spend most of the day with Tessie in Hoboken. She needs me now, Teddy."

"Of course, Hannah. We've got some time to practice and prepare." Teddy has been so understanding. He knows my heart is breaking for my friend.

It was the kind of news that no one wanted. After performing tests and consulting with other doctors, Uncle Ben has diagnosed Tessie with a brain tumor. Her headaches were a big clue, and the X-rays showed a small tumor on her brain. There is no cure, however there are some experimental treatments with radiation that could slow down the growth. Uncle Ben isn't sure if the treatments would be right for Tessie.

This news is the worst that I could imagine for my friend. To be so alive and vital, and now to learn that she has such a dreaded illness. A brain tumor? Life can change in an instant.

We don't know how long Tessie will live, but we want her time left to be as happy as we can make it. She doesn't know all the details about her condition. Simon wants to keep it that way, and I agree. The kids don't know too much either, but I think Alice may realize what's happening. We all try to shield Alvin from the truth. Let him remain happy and carefree for now.

Tessie doesn't leave the house much anymore. She has fallen a few times. The headaches are painful, and she is often confused. She takes special powders made in the drug store. Anacin and laudanum help sometimes. Simon and the children gently massage her forehead. She loves that.

I've prepared some food to bring to the house. Roast chicken and a kugel will be good because there will be leftovers. And, of course, mandel bread, to remind her of the good times, of all those talks in my kitchen before the diagnosis.

Today Uncle Ben drives me. He needs to make a house call to see Tessie in Hoboken, so we go together. I walk into the brownstone on 1235 Bloomfield Street with a feeling of anticipation and fear. What to expect? Tessie seems different with each visit. Which Tessie will I see today? Confused Tessie? Feisty Tessie? Poor me Tessie? I'm hoping for a calm Tessie.

*Barbara Pressman*

# "Poor Me" Tessie

After Uncle Ben examines her, Tessie waves me into her bedroom. She's been lying down, cold washcloth on her forehead. She's wearing her pink chenille bathrobe, and she wants to get up now. As we walk into the parlor, my eyes go to the winding polished wood banister that leads to the upstairs rooms for the boarders. I've seen Alvin slide down that bannister many times. Stained glass windows let in the light. A marble fireplace sits in the middle of the room.

"I love coming to your house Tessie. It's so warm and inviting. Your family is lucky to live in this brownstone."

"And what good is this house to me now? I feel useless. I need help walking. Alice does all the cooking. She makes breakfast for the boarders each morning. She and Simon clean the rooms upstairs. And my dreams of Alice marrying a rich man like Jake are over. I don't have enough energy to convince her. She tells me she's in love with Joe, the delivery boy. Simon even likes him now. Of course, he's going against my wishes, as always. Only Alvin listens to me. He's been writing poems for me. So sweet. And here I am, lying around all day, doing nothing. My life is over."

Tessie changes the subject. "How about you Hannah? Tell me about your job, about Teddy, and that selfish, *yenta* mother of his. I think she's too controlling. She wants to keep her son all to herself. It's not right."

"Well, you're right about that, Tessie. Teddy is the 'savior' of the family. They look to him for support, and I think they're afraid of losing him. But I really don't care. We love each other. Teddy spends lots of time with me, and the children. They adore him. He loves them too. We don't need to marry," I say with a smile.

"I'm not sure I believe you. What about Franny? Does she still want to go across the world to join Golda?"

"I'm happy to tell you that Franny is staying right here in New York after all. At least for now. I think I convinced her that she can do important work at home, helping to raise money for her Zionist causes.

"And there's more. A radio show wants to interview me about the *Help Me Hannah* column. It will happen in two weeks. I'm so nervous. Can I do it Tessie, do you think?"

"If I was well enough I would march right into that radio studio with you Hannah. You'll do a great job. What a great opportunity. Oy, and here I am sleeping all day, totally helpless. Why me? Why, dear God, I wish I knew. Your uncle says I'm doing fine, but I don't feel so fine."

I reach out and grab Tessie's hand. We stay like that, in silence. Strong, powerful silence.

# Radio Days

WOR studios are on Broadway, near Times Square. As we approach the building, I tell Teddy that I have butterflies in my stomach.

"Feeling a little nervous is a good thing, Hannah," Teddy tells me. We enter the building with its marble floors and high ceilings. "The adrenaline will enhance your performance," he says with a smile, squeezing my hand.

"And how would you know that dear Teddy? How many radio interviews have you done?" We stand close together as we enter the elevator. We practiced for this interview all day yesterday. I have notes and some examples of my advice letters in a folder.

I'm dressed in a mint green suit and a hat that Franny designed for me. It matches the suit perfectly. Not too fancy. Understated, but professional. I'm wearing my best pearls. On the radio, no one will see me, but looking good gives me confidence. My hair is shiny and smooth, my pompadour in place. Taking a deep breath, we march into the lobby of the WOR studios.

"We're here to see Mr. John Gambling. We have an appointment with him at 10:00," Teddy says, sounding very confident. I know Teddy by now. He's good at projecting authority. That's why people respect him.

The receptionist smiles, "Oh yes, I see that you are his first interview this morning. You will first see his assistant, Miss Irving. She will 'warm you up'. By the time Miss Irving is done with you, you'll be ready for anything," she says.

I think I like this place. With a sigh of relief, I can feel my body relaxing. The publicity will be so good for *The Jewish Gazette*. And for me. My heart starts to beat a little faster. "That's OK," I tell myself, taking Teddy's advice. Adrenaline.

After our warm up period, we're escorted into the recording studio. By now, I feel comfortable. The butterflies in my stomach have left. I'm actually looking forward to my 'time to shine'. I want to make everyone proud. I know my column has been interesting to our readers. Why not the radio audience too?

After the introduction and a little background, Mr. Gambling asks, "For those listeners who are unfamiliar with your column, Mrs. Altman, why don't you read one of the *Help Me Hannah* letters for our audience.

"First, please call me Hannah. And of course, I'd be happy to."

I take this carefully chosen letter out of my folder, take a deep breath, and read into the microphone.

*Hannah,*

*I hope you can help me. My problem concerns my husband. He has a good job as a house painter. He belongs to the Painter's Union too. He works hard all day and comes home very tired.*

*He has brought two of his brothers and one of his sisters over to the United States from Hungary. They each stayed with us in Jersey City until they could find a place of their own.*

*The youngest brother, Morris, was living with us for about a month. Morris is fun loving, handsome, and charming. My husband has always loved his younger brother, but not anymore. He didn't try very hard to find a job. Morris flirted with me quite a lot, and one time, when my husband was at work, he tried to kiss me. I was not comfortable with him being in the house after that. So, my husband asked him to leave. All day at work, he would wonder what might be happening at home. Maybe I was wrong to tell him about the kiss, but now it's too late.*

*After a heated argument, Morris left to go live with his other brother. When the other brother and his sister learned that my husband threw Morris out of our house, they were very angry with us. Of course, they've only heard Morris' side of the story. My husband tried to tell them the truth, but they didn't believe him. They believe only Morris, who claims his innocence. Now both brothers and the sister won't speak to us.*

*My husband was so sad about the rift that he went to visit them to try and reconnect. He walked up to the apartment, but they wouldn't let him in. His brother slammed the door in his face.*

*He came home to me, his face filled with rage and marked with tears.*

*"I brought them to America, I saved them. I gave them a new life. Someday they'll come to me," my husband said. But I'm not so sure that will happen.*

*Now my problem is this: Was it my fault? Now my husband has lost his dear brothers and sister. What can I do?*

*Sad Martha from Jersey City*

Mr. Gambling paused for just a moment, allowing radio silence to create a dramatic effect.

"My goodness," he said, "that's a complicated situation. How did you respond, Hannah?"

"Many family situations can be complicated, Mr. Grambling, and this one is even more complicated than usual. Here's how I responded to "Sad Martha.'

*Dear Martha,*

*It is not your fault. You were right to tell your husband about the way his brother acted when he wasn't home. It would have been wrong not to.*

*You must try to help. Go visit the brothers alone. Tell them how upset your husband is about the family rift. You should NOT bring up the attempted kiss. The younger brother has acted*

156

*deceitfully, but it's better left in the past. If they are receptive, invite them to visit your house.*

*I must warn you. The hurt on all sides may be too deep now. If they don't reunite, at least you know you have tried. There may be some bitter disappointment. But usually the truth wins in the end.*

Again, Mr. Grambling paused for affect and then asked, "I wonder whether our listeners would agree with your answer, Hannah. How do you decide what to write in response to these letters?"

Like Mr. Grambling, I waited for just a few seconds and then said, "I try to put myself in the position of the letter writers. I think about the emotions they must be feeling. I weigh all the possibilities in my response. People tell me that I'm quite intuitive, so usually the answers come pretty easily to me. I also want to be realistic. I can't give the readers hope when there is none, like today's letter."

I can see Teddy beaming from across the room.

When the interview ends, and we're off the air, Mr. Gambling thanks us and asks if I would consider coming back. Of course, Teddy and I both say yes.

"Teddy, I guess you're officially my agent now," I tease him. We walk out onto the street, holding hands and smiling as we take the subway to celebrate at Goldberg's. I can already picture us toasting, our glasses filled with Dr. Brown's cream soda.

# Champagne Anyone?

On Monday, when I walk into the newsroom my colleagues come over to congratulate me. They ask me how I felt during the radio interview.

"I was quite nervous at the beginning, but once I got started, I truly enjoyed myself," I answer.

They tell me it was a great show on Saturday morning and that the office phone lines have been ringing off the hook about the radio segment.

Teddy says, "I'll bet our *Help Me Hannah* letter entries will double after this radio publicity. And to think, it's all free advertising. We need to put your column in a more prominent spot now, with some good ads beside it. Our salesmen can use the success of the advice column to add to our profits. People love the human-interest stories that you bring to life with those letters, Hannah."

Teddy calls me aside. "I've been thinking, our celebration at Goldberg's Delicatessen wasn't really enough. Cream soda? No. We need to make a real toast, with champagne. Let's go uptown to the Cotton Club. We might even hear Duke Ellington's orchestra. Maybe Simon and Tessie will join us.

It will be a special night for the four of us. Your best friend should be there with you.

"I know you're wondering if we can afford it," Teddy continued. "Well, maybe *we* can't, but *The Jewish Gazette* can. A business expense, of course. And that includes paying for the Lesters."

"I love your idea, Teddy. I'm not sure if Simon would feel comfortable there, or if Tessie has the strength and balance to walk in," I say. I know Tessie would never go into a place like the Cotton Club using a cane. She would be humiliated. "Maybe if she holds on to Simon's and Teddy's arms," I say to myself.

"I am going to make it happen. Leave it to me. I have a plan," Teddy says confidently.

Why not just let it happen Teddy's way? He seems to be on top of the world these days, visibly happy. I know our being together contributes to that feeling.

Saturday night arrives. I'm wearing a royal blue silk dress, a little clingy, with patent leather shoes and an evening purse. Franny helped me pick out the outfit at the rental shop. She's got great taste, an eye for fashion.

Teddy picks me up in his borrowed Buick. "I feel like a million bucks," I beam at Teddy.

He looks and smells great. His curly black hair is neatly combed and shiny. It must be the *Brylcreem*.

"With a famous advice columnist and beautiful radio personality in the car with me, I feel like *two* million bucks," Teddy says, looking at me.

"Keep your eyes on the road or we'll never get to The Cotton Club," I tell him.

The plan is for Alice's boyfriend Joe to drive Simon and Tessie, so that we can meet there. And we'll take them home when the evening ends. A plan is just a plan. My nerves are on edge. With those two, plans don't always work out.

In the car, I ask Teddy how he talked Tessie into joining us. He tells me, "Easy. I told her it was a celebration for you Hannah, because of the radio segment. She couldn't resist, she's so proud of you. And how many times do people like us get to go to a nightclub? Tessie loved the idea. Simon was another story. He sat there, stone-faced when I suggested it. Tessie *sweet talked* him into it, and he reluctantly agreed, to please her, I'm sure. He's a gruff, strong man, but he loves his wife. No doubt about that."

Teddy is insightful about my friend and her husband. I tell Teddy how concerned I am about Tessie's health. "Each time I'm with her, she seems more confused, repeating herself, less steady on her feet. I also see that short, stocky body of hers become more frail, not quite as erect. She's lost a lot of weight. I'm just devastated about it, Teddy."

Teddy doesn't say anything. But his silence says a lot. We both know what's coming for my best friend. We know the inevitable.

I force my mind to go to happier thoughts. I don't want to ruin this night. We are both excited about the prospect of listening to the orchestra, and dancing too, a first for us. Just the thought of it makes my mood brighten. Teddy looks so handsome in his tuxedo, hair shiny and combed back, like one of those leading men we see in the movies. I give Teddy a gentle rub on his neck. He turns to me with that smile of his. The smile that tells me everything will be all right.

After we're seated, I look around. My eyes don't know where to begin. The huge dance floor is packed. I can't keep my eyes off the talented dancers doing the jitterbug. There are colorful murals on the walls and on the ceiling. The tables and booths are located all around the dance floor, for good viewing. Cab Calloway leads the orchestra tonight. His men are dressed in light blue suits and ties. The brass instruments shine. The energy of these musicians and dancers is electric.

The women are dressed in gowns, made of expensive, silk fabric and jewelry with dazzling, colored stones. The men look very rich, with gold cufflinks and pinky rings. One man has a ring with three large diamonds, which is all the rage now. It feels great to be here. The music makes us all part of one group of equals, each appreciating the talented horn players, drum rhythms and great vocals.

So where are Tessie and Simon? They should have been here 20 minutes ago. I start to get worried. Teddy takes my hand, calms me down. "This could all go terribly wrong," I think to myself. Those Lesters, tempers always flaring up. If they have an argument, Simon will refuse to come. Tessie will be furious. "Please, don't let this night be ruined," I pray.

Just then, I see Simon standing by the door, looking uncomfortable. Alice and her boyfriend Joe must have walked them to the door and left. Teddy and I get out of our chairs and walk over to greet them. We offer to help bring Tessie inside, but Simon shouts, "I can bring my own wife in myself. What kind of man do you think I am?" he says, pushing Teddy's arm away.

"Of course, Simon. I'm glad you're here with us." Teddy realizes Simon is a smoldering volcano. Simon proudly guides Tessie on his arm, until they reach our table, which is way in the back. The front seats are for the VIP set, of course. As they take their seats at our table, Simon gives us all a smug look.

"Let him be proud that he escorted his wife alone. He needs that tonight," I whisper to Teddy.

Just then the orchestra starts playing *I Only Have Eyes For You*. I start swaying in my seat, and Teddy puts out his hand. As he stands up, I follow him onto the dance floor. We seem to fit together perfectly. Our bodies move in perfect precision with the music. "It all feels so easy, so right," I think, as that warm glow comes back whenever we're together. I'm upset when the song ends. Later, I tell myself. Later when we're alone.

Tessie wants to dance but Simon won't hear of it. He frowns and stares into space. Even the music doesn't seem to move him. It's easy to see that Tessie is disappointed—and angry.

When the waiter comes to our table, Teddy orders champagne all around. We hold up our glasses and toast the *Help Me Hannah* column and the radio interview. Teddy continues, "Here's to good friends and good health. And most of all, here's to our very own advice columnist, Hannah Altman."

"Thank you, Teddy. And thank you Tessie and Simon for honoring us with your company." Oh, this night is magical. I'm beaming. I can't help myself.

Simon tastes the champagne, makes a face, and remarks, "I like schnapps better." Tessie gives him a look. We all smile, then laugh, even Simon. The ice is broken.

At midnight, we drive the Lesters home. Tessie is talkative in the car, and she thanks Teddy for treating them to this very special evening. Simon is quiet, but we know he enjoyed himself, in his own way. When we pull up to 1235 Bloomfield Street, Tessie says *"Zay Gezunt.* Drive carefully and get home safely you two."

"See you on Saturday, Tessie," I reply. Simon guides Tessie inside without any help, very slowly, and so very tenderly. Tessie walks in safely. Simon takes the role of protector quite seriously. As they open the front door, we wave, relieved. Now it's time to go back to my apartment, and that's where we finish what we started on the dance floor.

# A Poet Among Us

As a promotion for *The Jewish Gazette,* the staff decides to run a contest. More and more, Teddy realizes that human interest features are making the paper very popular. We consult with a few teacher friends who help us promote a poetry contest for school children. It's Spring, and a perfect time for our topic: Mother's Day. Children are invited to write a poem to honor their mothers. Because I have been assigned to oversee the Women's Page, I've been asked to place the ad for the newspaper contest.

*Calling all Student Poets ages 6-18*

*The Jewish Gazette is looking for talented children to write a poem about their mothers. We will grant first, second, and third prizes. Each winner will receive a monetary award.*

*First place-$15*

*Second place-$10*

*Third place-$5*

*Your poem will be printed in the Sunday edition of the paper. Please submit your poems by April 30th. Your poem must be written in your best penmanship. Be sure to include a self- addressed, stamped envelope to receive your prize money. If you're one of our lucky winners, your poem will appear in the Sunday edition, on Mother's Day.*

*Good luck to all.*

It's Saturday, and I'm on my way to Hoboken. There's a chill in the air, and I'm glad I brought my warm jacket. I bring mandel bread with me, wrapped tightly in tin foil. On the ferry, I think about my job at the Gazette. I love answering my *Help Me Hannah* letters. My advice comes pretty easily. I'm glad I've been given more responsibility. The poetry contest should be interesting.

My mind wanders to Tessie. With each visit, my fears increase. Sometimes she surprises me with her strength, and sometimes my worst fears are realized. "Oy, why dear God? Please give me the strength to know what to say, to be positive. Let her have some happiness during this time of declining health," I say to myself.

Today, when Simon opens the door, he greets me with a look of doom. "Tessie fell again this morning Hannah. She's in bed now. I want she should be alone, but she got mad when I said that. I will let you visit anyway," Simon says, with rounded shoulders and his head bent slightly downward.

I sit on a chair next to Tessie's bed. My eyes go to a chamber pot next to her, because she might fall if she walks to the bathroom. The thought of my friend needing one of those is upsetting.

"Tessie, let me get us some tea on a tray and we can each have a piece of mandel bread to dunk," I say, trying to sound cheerful.

"Alice, come here please. We need your help." Alice joins us, and I tell her the plan for our little bedside tea party. We go together to the big kitchen in the basement. Alice catches me up while we prepare the tray.

"Mrs. Altman, my boyfriend Joe and I are helping Father with his cleaning business, and it's going very well." She beams with pride. And Alvin is doing better in school. We try not to worry him about Mother's condition. I know you are worried about her, but I have things under control," she assures me.

I like hearing those words from Alice. She is a wonderful daughter. And now that Simon has a steady income, he must feel more secure also. He needs to have some pride now. Hard times are ahead for the Lester family. We all know it.

Once I'm settled at Tessie's bedside, I fill her in about my family news. I know the distraction will help.

"Let's see Tessie. Where do I begin?" I ask. "Solly is very happy about something. He got the part in the play in the Jewish Center. They needed a few older children. He's been practicing his small part faithfully. And he never stutters. Franny is doing very well in school and working part time in a hat shop. I'm proud of both of them."

"So, *nu*, Hannah, what about you and Teddy? No plans yet for a wedding? It's that mother of his. I know it. Teddy must be afraid of her. What kind of grown man is afraid of his mother?" Leave it to Tessie to be blunt. Her words hurt. Deep down I know they are true.

Tessie continues, "Let me have a talk with him. And with his mother. I need to make things right for you before I leave this earth." Her eyes well up with tears. This is the first time she expressed her fate. Now I'm holding back my tears.

"Let's talk about something nice," I say. "Teddy has put me in charge of a contest for children at *The Jewish Gazette*. It's a poetry contest for Mother's Day. I think Alvin should enter. He loves to write."

"Oy, what a good idea, Hannah. My boy is brilliant, a creative dreamer. Oh, he'll love to write a poem about me. He always tells me how much he loves me. My children are the reason I want to go on living, Hannah. Now, just the little things, like watching them as they sleep, are so special for me. Just plain, everyday things." More tears for both of us.

On the trip home, I have a heavy heart. I hope Tessie has some time left with us. And I hope she doesn't suffer too much. I try to focus my mind on the Poetry Contest.

Sure enough, five days after my Hoboken visit, an envelope appears on my desk, from Bloomfield Street. Alvin has sent me his illustrated poem. Two pages - one the poem written in his best cursive penmanship, the other a picture drawn with crayon, to accompany his masterpiece.

### My Day at the Beach with Mother by Alvin Lester

*It's early Sunday morning,*
*Off to the beach we go,*
*Mother invites some friends along,*
*Kids from the street we know.*

*We take the subway and a train,*
*To the water and blue sky,*
*We hope that fun awaits us,*
*As the time goes slowly by.*

*Mother holds my hand so tight,*
*As we walk along the shore,*
*Looking left and looking right.*
*We take in more and more.*

*With careful eyes Mom watches us,*
*Kids jump and swim and play,*
*Until it's time to eat our lunch,*
*On the blanket not far away.*

*Out come the egg sandwiches,*
*And lemonade so sweet,*
*We are so very hungry,*
*We all dig in and eat.*

*When the sky begins to darken,*
*We leave feeling tired and calm,*
*That's when I say to myself,*
*Alvin…. you've got the greatest Mom.*

Our team of judges include two English teachers, two journalists, and of course, me. We had over one hundred entries. Alvin Lester was the winner of the second-place prize. Maybe I helped influence the decision, just a little, but the others agreed. The Lester family *qvelled* for weeks. Alvin was in seventh heaven. Both the poem and announcement of the prize are both framed and hanging up in the parlor, right next to the picture of FDR, of course.

# A Cousin in the House

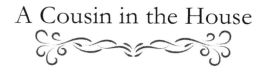

As her condition worsens, it's obvious that Tessie's tumor continues spreading. Uncle Ben says he's not sure if a cure is possible. Some experimental treatments, like radiation, may not help Tessie. Her case is quite advanced. Yet she continues to be the head of the household on 1235 Bloomfield Street. At least she thinks she is. Simon and the kids allow her to feel that way.

Tessie repeats herself a lot. At times she's as feisty as ever. Uncle Ben thinks she has had a few small strokes. She has weakness on her left side. Sometimes her words are slurred.

When I arrive on Saturday morning, Tessie's wearing makeup and her hair is shiny and combed. The strong scent of *Evening in Paris* fills the bedroom. I haven't seen *this Tessie* for a long time. "How nice to see you looking so lovely, my friend," I tell her.

"I can't wait for you to meet my cousin Richard Schlesinger. He arrived on Wednesday. HIAS helped him find us. I barely remember him from the old country. Somehow, he got false papers and fled from Budapest. He'll stay in one of the upstairs rooms. Right now, he's too weak to look for work. Hannah, he's so quiet. Very shy, and very handsome. Of course, he's quite a few years younger than me." Tessie says, with a little smile, looking down at her lap.

As Tessie was talking, I thought about the wonderful work that the Hebrew Immigrant Aid Society—HIAS—has done. They've been around since the 1800s and were invaluable in helping so many European immigrants resettle in the United States after they fled the pogroms. They're continuing to help now.

Just then, Richard walks into the room. He is slight, with reddish brown hair. In her sweetest voice, Tessie introduces us. He doesn't speak much English yet, but with a little Yiddish we manage to talk. Alice has been giving him a few basic language lessons, Tessie informs me.

I tell him it's nice to meet him and he proudly replies in his thick accent, "*Likevise, I'm sure.*" He shyly waves and walks out the front door.

Tessie whispers to me, "Richard has met our neighbor, Irene Kilcullen. She seems to have a crush on him. They like to sit on the stoop together. She's from a lovely Irish family. Let them be friends; it will be good for Richard. What's the harm?"

Tessie continues, "I heard that you were invited back to WOR for another radio show. Dr. Ben told me last week."

"Yes, and I'm really excited. Teddy and I are going to practice at his house tomorrow. Mr. Gambling wants to consider me for a regular spot with the network," I reveal.

"Good money too, Tessie. Now I might even have enough to make a generous contribution to my little *Tzedukah* box every week. "

"Hmmm going to Teddy's house? Will that wicked woman be there?" I know where Tessie is going with this. She's not happy that Teddy and I haven't gotten married. She's convinced Mrs. Damsky is keeping us apart. And I know she's right. Do I have the strength to take him away from his mother and sisters who depend on him?

"I can't worry about it now, Tessie. I'm ok with the way things are. I'm taking good care of myself and my kids on my own."

"From your mouth to God's ears, Hannah. It should only stay that way, *poo poo*. Me? I need more help from God these days. I've been forgetting things. I've been having fainting spells too. One time, Cousin Richard found me on the bathroom floor and helped me back to bed. I hope he stays with us a while."

I hold her hand and we stay that way, in silence. Let Tessie have a little joy, a little fantasy, maybe a tiny crush on Richard. Simon will never know. It will be our secret.

# Hiatal Hernia

I bake rugelach to bring to Teddy's mother and sisters. I decide against sponge cake. Surely it won't be fluffy enough. Maybe the buttery sweetness of the cookies will ease the tension a little. Mildred and Evelyn thank me. But Mrs. Damsky gives me her usual half-hearted smile. No words of thank you, of course. I can tell that the sisters are embarrassed because they go overboard with their compliments.

"Oh, you always make wonderful baked goods, Hannah," Mildred says. Mrs. Altman lets out a groan.

"What's wrong Mom?" Teddy asks.

"It's my hiatal hernia again, *mein* darling son. Oy, I can't get any relief. I better not eat any of Hannah's cookies. It will only make things worse, all that sugar and butter." She looks up at me, in slow motion. I ignore her comment.

While having our tea and rugelach, Teddy and I settle down to work. I begin to cough a bit. The tea went down the wrong way. Teddy gets all flustered. Mildred and Evelyn ask if I'm all right.

"I'm fine everyone. I probably drank too fast. A glass of water is all I need," I say. I take a deep breath and smile. "See? I'm ok now."

Mrs. Damsky stands up abruptly, her face red with rage. "I could be lying on the floor dead, and no one would notice. But Hannah? She just belches, and you all go running to her." With that she walks into the bedroom and slams the door.

Teddy goes in to see her. He closes the door. I hear shouting from inside. Then Teddy comes out slowly.

He sits down beside me and says, "Hannah, I want to apologize for my mother. She has no manners. She was rude and unkind. And I let her know that." I wonder if this is the first time he's ever spoken up to his mother. Teddy almost looks happy, empowered, relieved.

I take Teddy's hand in mine. My instincts tell me it's better not to say anything. Instead, he speaks. "My mother needed to hear that. She can't continue to control my life. I deserve to be happy, Hannah. I've been silent for much too long."

The sisters observe, looking concerned. They depend on Teddy too. After all, Mildred is a piano teacher and Evelyn stays home to take care of her mother. Their income is terribly small.

"Why don't we go outside for a walk, Teddy," I suggest. We grab our coats, hold hands, and leave. Teddy doesn't even say goodbye. Once we're safely out on the sidewalk, Teddy opens up.

"Ever since my father died, I've been the head of the household. They depend on me for everything. I pay the bills, I take them shopping, take them to shul, I fix things, I settle arguments. Until I met you, I never cared. Can't these women see how much I love you?" He pulls me close and we kiss, not caring who sees us. All the sounds and sights of the street fall away. Right now, we are the only two people in the world.

"Let's go to my house and finish our practice session. We need to be ready for tomorrow," I say. Back in Washington Heights, we walk into my apartment. The kids are out. Lucky for us. Teddy and I embrace, clothes come off, and he guides me to the sofa, touching every part of my body, slowly this time. We appreciate the wonders that await us. All the emotion from the afternoon washes away in our lovemaking. When we are finished, we lie together, taking it all in, without speaking.

Just then I start to laugh. "What about the practice session, Teddy?"

He answers, "Who cares? We can work all evening. I'm not going home. This is my home now, Hannah. With you and your children."

# Help Me Hannah # 11

Dear Hannah,

*I am a 25-year old man. I came to Chicago after leaving my village in Russia. I have been working in my cousin's butcher shop. I do not enjoy my work at all.*

*I have a friend who told me about an opportunity to buy a farm in North Dakota. He went there with his wife and bought a small farm last year. He told me that he grows potatoes and raises chickens. They have all the butter and cheese that they need. I went to visit them and I loved my time there. I helped my friend with his work. He said I would make a great farmer myself. He said he would help me get started.*

*I went back to Chicago and told my friends about my plan to be a farmer in North Dakota. They called me an idiot. They can't believe a capable Jewish man would give up the city life and go be a farmer. What Jewish girl would ever marry me?*

*But I am not discouraged. I want to follow my dream of being a farmer.*

*Hannah, are my friends right? Am I an idiot for wanting a country type of life? Will I ever find a wife to join me?*

*Thank you,*

*A Jewish Farmer*

· · · · · · ·

*Dear Jewish Farmer,*

*You are an independent thinker. You have nothing to be ashamed of. City people and country people each think they have the best life.*

*In the city, people suffer from all sorts of diseases, such as Tuberculosis. Most farmers are strong and healthy. Many live seventy years or more. If you love the country life, join your friend. I am sure there will be a woman who shares your love of nature. Maybe your friend's wife knows of someone for you.*

*I encourage you to pursue your dream.*

# A Test

Teddy and I arrive at the radio studios of WOR, bright and early on Thursday morning. John Gambling's assistant guides us in. She says, "Hannah, you did so well last time, you really don't need coaching. Mr. Gambling will be ready for you in about thirty minutes. Why don't the two of you relax? The format will basically be the same. I'll get you some coffee."

While we wait, I review the *Help Me Hannah* letters from my folder, preparing my verbal answers. I like to expand on them for the listening audience, to give insight into the letter writers' backgrounds. Some of the Jewish Immigrants' problems may not be of interest to the general New York audience.

Teddy sits by my side, more for moral support than anything else. A few minutes later, John Gambling appears.

"Hello Hannah and Mr. Damsky," John says, shaking hands. "Please, follow me so that we can do a sound check, just like last time. Hannah, I have a plan. We've asked staff members, family members, and friends of the network to submit problems of their own, anonymously of course. They were very happy for the opportunity to seek your advice. I want to see if you can think on your feet. I didn't warn you on purpose."

My heart begins to pound. Teddy sees my face flush and he suggests that I take a few deep breaths. We both know I can do this, but it will certainly be a challenge. I'm sure this is some kind of test. "Here we go," I say to myself as I put on a smile.

The on-air light illuminates and Mr. Gambling begins to speak into the microphone. "Good morning listening audience. Rambling With Gambling here. We have a return guest today, our very own Hannah Altman, the advice columnist from *The Jewish Gazette*. Our listeners have submitted questions to her."

He continues. "Our first question is from a young professional woman. Hannah Altman is seeing this letter for the first time. She'll read the letter to you and give her advice.

I take the letter and begin reading.

*Dear Hannah,*

*I hope you can help me with a delicate problem. My boyfriend is a great guy. He's handsome, funny, and well-liked. My family and my friends love him. He is an excellent salesman, and travels quite a bit to visit clients.*

*A few times I've caught him in lies. I heard him telling stories to different people, and changing parts of the same story. Each change makes him sound more successful, more important.*

*I don't want to humiliate him. I have never challenged him in front of others. But I would like to ask him about it when we're alone.*

*I like this man and enjoy his company. Do I have a future with him?*

*Signed,*

*Honest Ann*

I pause for just a moment to collect my thoughts. Should I be direct or circumspect? Should I give good advice or something that the audience might want to hear instead? I make my decision.

"Ann, this man may be very charming. He's probably fun to be with, salesmen usually are. But once a liar, always a liar. It's okay to question him when his story isn't consistent. If he doesn't come clean about the lies, then you have your answer. If you get involved with a liar, you will be the one to lose. Don't lie to yourself. You deserve to be with someone you can trust."

I can tell by the look on Mr. Gambling's face—Teddy's too, that my first try at this type of Q and A was quite satisfactory. We continue the pattern for the next hour. The questions are interesting to me. They're from different types of people than the readers of the Jewish Gazette. But human nature doesn't change, I've noticed, no matter what.

At the end of the hour, Mr. Gambling signs off. "That's it for today's program. Thank you, Hannah for your enlightening answers. I'm sure our friends out there in WOR land enjoyed today's show. Signing off for now, this is John Gambling."

When the mics are off, we all take a deep breath. John excuses himself for a moment. When the door opens again, the head of the station walks in. He tells me that WOR would like to offer me a weekly program, giving advice, just as we did today.

He smiles as he says, "Hannah, don't make any decisions right now. We'll write up a proposal and send it to you, care of *The Jewish Gazette*. I hope to call you my colleague very soon," John Gambling says, with a warm smile. Teddy and I are escorted into the lobby, and try to look professional. But I, for one, am ready to burst out of there, kick my heels together and jump for joy.

We walk into the Horn and Hardart Automat on 42nd Street and I find a table and sit down. I tell Teddy to wait. "Today's lunch is my treat," I tell him. I come back to the table with two plates of piping hot macaroni and cheese and two pieces of apple pie.

Teddy raises his glass and toasts the moment. "Here's to new beginnings. I have something I want to give you Hannah. I've been waiting for the right moment, but I can't wait any longer."

He reaches into his pocket and takes out an opal ring, in a lovely gold setting. "I can't afford a diamond right now, but please accept this opal ring as a symbol of our engagement. Let's make it official. Hannah, please marry me."

# Jelly Milk

"Good morning fiancé." I say the next morning, as I snuggle into Teddy's side. It's great not waking up alone. Having Teddy with me in the morning is a luxury that I can't seem to get enough of. The kids are comfortable with Teddy now. After all, we are engaged to be married.

As I get out of bed, Teddy says, "Not just yet Hannah, please. Let's stay awhile." He pulls me back. But there are noises in the hallway.

"Mom, I'm soooo hungry," Solly shouts.

It's Sunday morning and the kids are used to a big breakfast. I throw on my bathrobe and go to the kitchen. Today I'm going to make one of their favorites, a jelly omelet. Teddy gives me a hand, setting the table. He admires my technique of pouring the whipped-up eggs into a sizzling buttered frying pan.

"Please take out the strawberry jelly from the ice box Solly. And wake up your sister. Breakfast will be ready soon."

I scrape out the last of the strawberry jelly and fill the omelets. Then I pour milk into the almost empty jelly jar. I shake the jar and pour the frothy pink mixture into little glasses.

"What are you doing, Hannah?" Teddy asks. I explain the history of our *jelly milk*. "When Abe was alive, this was his specialty. We were always stretching our pennies. *Jelly milk* was our way of getting every last drop. And the kids love it. It's our variation on chocolate milk."

"Clever idea. Abe must have been a great father. I hope your kids will accept me as their stepfather," Teddy says with a little unease in his voice.

The kids sit down at the table. Franny must have overheard our conversation, because she looks up and says, "Welcome to our family." Solly walks over to Teddy and, with a big grin, shakes his hand.

Teddy and I are relieved, but that's just the start. How will Teddy's mother and sister take the news? And of course, there's Tessie. I think she'll be thrilled for me. How about the staff at *The Jewish Gazette*? And my parents and brother? Where will we have the wedding? Who will we invite?

For now, I won't let anyone or anything steal my happiness. As long as my children approve of Teddy and I, nothing else matters.

# Recipe for Jelly Milk

It's more likely the foam and sweetness that does the trick, but I've never met a small child who doesn't like this pink concoction better than regular milk.

**Take an almost empty jelly jar**
**Fill with milk**
**Shake vigorously until milk turns pink and foamy**

Serve in little glasses to smiling faces.

# It's Official

> *Announcement of Marriage*
>
> *We are happy to announce that Hannah Altman and Theodore Damsky were married in a private ceremony on August 20, 1936. The happy couple resides in Washington Heights, New York. We thank our family and friends for their kind wishes.*

It's Saturday, and today I'm bringing Teddy with me for my Hoboken visit. Tessie wanted to come to the wedding, but our decision to have a private ceremony made that impossible. But why not have a little celebration in Hoboken with the Lesters?

Alice bought some apple strudel for the occasion. Alvin wrote a wedding poem, and Simon gave us a bottle of his homemade wine. Cousin Richard shook hands with Teddy and gave me a shy little kiss. A lovely red headed young woman is standing next to Richard. I've never seen her before.

"Who is this, Richard?" I ask.

Richard says, "This is *mein* friend, Irene."

"Ah, you must live next door. Are you a Kilcullen? Tessie talks to me about your family sometimes. So nice to meet you," I tell her.

"Thank you, Mrs….?" Oooops, I just remembered my new married name. "Sorry Irene, I just got married. My name is Hannah Damsky now. This is my husband, Teddy Damsky.

"A pleasure to meet you both," Irene says. Then she gives Richard a nudge.

*"Likevise, gut to meet you,"* Richard says, bravely entering the conversation. Irene beams at him. Richard seems proud of himself too. They wave goodbye, and go outside to sit on the front stoop.

Tessie says, "My head again, I need to lie down. Hannah, will you keep me company?"

I ask Teddy if he would mind. I hesitate to leave him alone with Simon. I hope he will be able to make conversation with him. He gives me his 'it's okay' look. Teddy is one of those people who can talk with anyone. It's one of the things I love about him. He's a real *mensch*.

Once Tessie is settled in bed, head propped up on two pillows, she checks to see if anyone can hear. "What do you think about Richard and Irene? She's a nice girl, yes. But for Richard? Come on Hannah. It's just wrong. I worry that they may be more than friends."

"Let poor Richard have someone to talk to, even *a very special* someone," I say. Of course, even now, Tessie is running the lives of all of her family members. I wonder if Tessie might be just a little jealous. "What harm can it be?" I comment.

"Plenty Hannah, and you know it." Even now, you can't get anything past her.

"Never mind then. I know what's going on with those two." Tessie continues, "Anyway, *Mazel Tov* on your marriage. I'm very happy for you. But why didn't you invite Simon and me? Was that asking so much to have your best friend at your wedding? What little joy I get now, it would have been a *mitzvah* for me to be there."

"I think you know why Tessie. With all the complications on Teddy's side of the family, we thought it best to have our wedding ceremony totally private. Only the children, Teddy and I. We went to Rabbi Halpern's study. It was a beautiful ceremony for us. Short and simple, just the way we like it. And no worries that his mother would make a scene."

Tessie gives me a look. "That woman would have given you the evil eye. She could have ruined your day. She must know you are married by now."

"Well, after the notice appeared in the newspaper, there could be no more secrets. Teddy and I went to his family. I suggested we stop at Wolf's bakery and bring flowers and some pastries as a peace offering. We told them about our private wedding. Mildred and Evelyn congratulated us with hugs all around. His mother behaved as we expected she would. She barely looked at either of us, cold as ice. But she can't stay mad at us forever. She needs Teddy's love and support."

Tessie reacted by saying, "She better come around or she'll lose her son completely. What a *meshugana*. Maybe you'll have two nice sisters-in-law."

I answered, "I hope so. They are nice ladies, just like Teddy. How could that woman have raised such good human beings? Mildred and Evelyn love my kids. They seem happy to have the family enlarged."

Tessie doesn't answer. To my surprise, her eyes are closed. She's fallen asleep. My signal to exit. I kiss her on the forehead and tiptoe out of the room. Teddy and I say our goodbyes to the family and walk out to the front stoop.

Cousin Richard and Irene are sitting together holding hands. They quickly stand up, quite flustered, Richard's ruddy complexion is even more flushed than usual. Tessie was right, they are more than friends. We arrive home and I try not to think about Teddy's mother. I'm also concerned about Tessie, and how she fell asleep. Simon said that Tessie sleeps most of the day now. Maybe it's for the best. I need to ask Uncle Ben.

Before going to bed, I look through my *Help Me Hannah* letters— always a good distraction for me. This one might be a good choice for the radio show.

# Help Me Hannah # 12

*Dear Hannah,*

*My widowed mother has been in a wheelchair for most of my life. I have two brothers who got married and moved to Jersey. I have a job as a secretary for a dress company and make pretty good wages, enough to support us both.*

*My mother doesn't appreciate the sacrifice I have made. She says it's a daughter's duty to take care of her mother. She would be all alone if I weren't around. She can do many things for herself, but of course she needs my support. Sometimes I feel guilty when I leave the house.*

*As you can see, the burden falls on me. My brothers' wives do nothing. My brothers visit once in a while. They count on me for everything with Mother. I see no way out, no future. Even if I go on dates or have a boyfriend, who would want me? The man would have to marry me AND my wheelchair-bound mother. So, I don't even join clubs or go out with my coworkers.*

*I've given up on life. I see no way out. And no one cares. Sometimes I want to end it all.*

*From,*

*Desperate*

. . . . . . .

*Dear Desperate,*

*You are feeling sorry for yourself. And you're being a martyr. You have a family. They don't help because you allow that.*

*You have a responsibility for sure. And yes, it feels like a burden. But you must talk to your brothers and their wives. Be open about your feelings. They should understand that you need your own time and your own life.*

*Set up a schedule for your brothers and their wives. You should oversee which days they visit. They must shop for her and help cover expenses. They must help with her companionship.*

*Your future can be bright if you let it. You must have a social life. Go out with friends after work. Go to movies with friends. Join a club. The possibilities are endless.*

*If you don't do these things, you will be a bitter young woman. You don't deserve that.*

# A Tzimmes

Uncle Ben has some free time for me today at 4:00 in the office. Aunt Rose, back in her role, greets me in the waiting room. She congratulates me on the marriage, and the *Help Me Hannah* radio show. I ask about little Michael.

"Michael is doing very well, Hannah. The nanny loves him. And she does light housework, even gets supper started for me. She is a blessing for our family, such a help. Our doctor's office, with me back, is running smoothly again. The regulars ask for you, sometimes. I appreciate that you took my place when I needed you."

I guess that's a compliment, but I'm not too sure. Aunt Rose will always be Aunt Rose. The job gave me a start. For that I am grateful.

Uncle Ben greets me with a big hug. "We've missed you Hannah," he says with a warm smile. I hope Aunt Rose heard him.

"Please tell me about my friend Tessie. She's been sleeping a lot lately. What does that mean?" I ask.

"Her cancer is advancing. The tumor is growing but slowly. No one can predict how much time she has left. Your

Barbara Pressman

concern is justified. I wish I could be more positive. I'm hoping advances in radiation might help her. Right now, probably not. But Tessie has a will to live. That works in her favor. I'm sure your friendship means a great deal."

"Thank you, dear Uncle. Someday soon we will stop by for a visit. We all want to see how much Michael has grown. Goodbye Uncle Ben."

Back at home that same evening Teddy tells me that his sister Mildred has invited us to their apartment for Passover seder. Teddy says, "I have always read from the Haggadah and led the service. It would be hard for them to have a seder without me. Maybe this will be a 'truce' with Mother. What do you think? Should we say yes?"

I give it some thought. "It will be an insult if we don't go Teddy. Although your mother has not made things easy for us, families should be together for holidays. God willing, your sisters will smooth the way. It will be nice for the kids too. I'll have Solly practice the Four Questions. I'll bring a carrot tzimmes. Franny will be a big help. Let's hope for a pleasant evening."

This morning, I'm making the carrot tzimmes. It smells wonderful, simmering on the stove. I added some extras to the usual carrots and sweet potatoes. This time I included prunes, a little sautéed onion, and some honey—sweet and savory. What could be bad?

While I'm cooking, Teddy walks in and says, "You're a real *balabusta,* Hannah."

While the tzimmes is on the stove, Solly and Frances are working on the four questions. Franny says, "Solly, if you get nervous or stuck on a word, just pretend that you're reciting lines from a show. Just look at me and I'll give you a sign."

Teddy tells me that he's been sending money to his mother and sisters each week. He stopped by once for a visit a few days ago. Tempers seem to have cooled down, which explains the invitation. He told his mother that there will be no rude outbursts this time. I wonder if she will take those words to heart.

When we arrive, the sisters welcome us. Teddy's mother stays in the background. Solly enthusiastically tries to say hello, but he stammers. The stutter seems to come out during times like these. His face turns red. Teddy's mother whispers to me, "You know Hannah, when a mother goes to work, the children sometimes develop nervous tics, for example, a stutter."

Franny overhears, and tells her, "Solly started stuttering way before my mother went to work. We're both proud and happy about Mom's job. Solly will be just fine. You don't have to worry, Mrs. Damsky. I've been helping my brother. He gets better and better each day. But some days are harder for him. That's all."

Mrs. Damsky walks away. Teddy gives Franny a knowing smile. I just love that daughter of mine. She's becoming quite the diplomat.

As the seder begins, a warm glow of togetherness permeates the room. New beginnings for our families. Teddy reads from the *Haggadah*, we say our blessings and drink our wine. It's time for the Four Questions.

Teddy says, "Solly, since you're the youngest male, please read the Four Questions for us."

All eyes are on my son. I feel my heart beating in my chest. "Please God, let him get through this," I say to myself.

"*Mmmmmah, Nish Ta Naaaaa.*" Solly is struggling, just as I feared. He stops, takes a breath. He waits. He glances at his sister, who holds her head high and looks at Solly with a nod of confidence. After a moment of hesitation, my son begins again, this time flawlessly, with a strong voice, perfect Hebrew, perfect pitch. We are all rooting for him. When he completes his part, I beam at him proudly. Even though it's not customary, we all give a little clap of approval. Solly laughs with relief.

Teddy reads every prayer and we sing every song. Yes, every single prayer on every single page. I keep wishing he would skip a page or two. Abe used to do that. Not Teddy. By the time we eat, the kids and I are starving. While the sisters, Franny and I serve, Mrs. Damsky is shouting out her orders,

"Be sure to put three matzoh balls in Teddy's soup. He's looking awfully thin these days."

Once we're all seated, and eating the steaming soup, Franny announces, "Next year in Jerusalem has special meaning for me now."

Teddy's sister Evelyn asks, "Why is that Frances?"

Franny goes on to tell the family about her relationship with Golda Meir and the invitation to help settle Jewish children fleeing the pogroms in Europe. "Golda wants me to work on a kibbutz. It sounds wonderful, but I can't go just yet. I need money for travel. My Youth Group might help me. Mom thinks I'm too young. I know I'll get there someday. I've been saving money from my job at the hat shop."

"That sounds dangerous Franny. Are you sure you want to travel that far from home?" Mrs. Damsky asks.

"I'm very sure Mrs. Damsky, when the time is right. We've all heard about what's going on in Europe and it's only getting worse. Adolph Hitler and his followers have too much power. I need to help my Jewish brothers and sisters. The kibbutz will provide a safety for our people. There is strength in numbers. Everyone works together on a kibbutz, doing all the jobs. They grow their own food. It's my dream to be there."

Solly, not to be ignored, talks about school and his plays. He's proud of being the star of his school plays, and the current production of *Tevye, The Dairy Man* at the Jewish

Community Center. Teddy and I tell the ladies about our work with *The Jewish Gazette*. And Evelyn announces that she got a job, working at the Crown Corset Factory. This is a happy surprise. Mildred listens with great interest, smiling proudly.

When the meal is done, after we sing *Chad Gad Ya,* Teddy and I, along with two sleepy kids, head to the door. Mrs. Damsky gives each of my children a little package of Passover Jelly fruit slices and macaroons. The cool spring air hits our faces as we step outside, walking to the subway stop. Teddy and I cling to each other, tighter than ever. I say to him, "I hope that extra matzah ball will fatten you up. And next time, we wouldn't mind if you skip a page or two."

Teddy laughs, "It's nice to have such a critic. When we get home, we can see if that extra matzah ball has given me strength for my other *husbandly* duties.

"You'll need that young man, I promise you," I respond.

# Recipe for Carrot Tzimmes

I save this dish for holidays. Rosh Hashanah and Passover are a perfect time for Tzimmes. The longer your bake, the better it tastes. Although some of the dish is made on top of the stove, it finishes in the oven. Many people add raisins too. You can add or subtract the ingredients to your taste.

**10 carrots peeled and sliced**
**4 sweet potatoes**
**2 T oil or chicken fat**
**1 onion**
**A handful of prunes**
**1/2 cup apricot preserves**
**1 cup orange juice**
**Sprinkle of cinnamon**
**½ cup honey**
**½ cup brown sugar**

Preheat oven to 350 degrees. Cook carrots and sweet potatoes in boiling water until tender. Drain. Reserve some liquid.
Saute chopped onion in skillet until brown. Now add prunes and continue cooking 10 minutes more. Stir in orange juice, preserves, cinnamon, brown sugar, and honey. Put carrots and sweet potatoes in a baking dish, then add prune mixture. Bake for 30 minutes. Add reserved liquid. Continue baking until carrots are tender, about 15 more minutes.

# Help Me Hannah Letter # 13

*Dear Hannah,*

*My husband and I have been happily married for over 25 years. We are not very religious. We are freethinkers and Zionists. We have four wonderful children. We gave them all a good education. Two of them went to City College. One works in a department store. Our youngest daughter is 21-years old and graduated from college with honors, but she couldn't find work. Two months ago, she got a very good job with an insurance company. She brings home $35.00 a week, which helps our household greatly.*

*My husband is very upset because the only way she got her job was to give her religion as Episcopalian on the application. She would never have gotten the job if they knew she was Jewish. She's fair skinned, and doesn't really look Jewish. My son told me that she got a letter of recommendation from a minister as proof to assure the boss that he was not being fooled.*

*Our house is divided now. I feel that our daughter hasn't committed a crime. Would it be better if she had to depend on us for every dollar? I sympathize with my daughter. But my husband is very concerned and insists that she should give up the job.*

*We would like your opinion Hannah. What should we do?*

*Signed,*

*Your Troubled Readers*

• • • • • • •

*Dear Troubled Readers,*

*I understand your distress. I believe your daughter was wrong to deceive her boss about her religion. It is wrong for companies to discriminate against Jews for employment. I'm sure they have plenty of Jewish clients and would never turn away their business.*

*It's fair to tell your daughter how you feel. But she is 21 and has a right to do what she feels she must do to earn a living. She is not alone. You can't stop her. She has a right to act as she wishes.*

# Friendship

It's been a busy week. Observing Passover falls to me, keeping the house free of bread and flour products. I make matzoh brei each morning for breakfast. The kids love it with a little sugar on top. Teddy goes along with them, but I use salt and pepper instead.

We went to shul together as a family. I was proud to have Teddy by my side. I saw some whispers. They all knew Abe quite well. He was a *macher* in our shul, past president. If people talk, I really don't care. Once they get to know Teddy, they will understand. And should I be alone for the rest of my life? Franny and I wore our best outfits and prettiest hats, Franny's creations, of course. Solly proudly sat with Teddy in the men's section.

Then a busy week at the paper and planning for the radio program. I've gotten good feedback about it. WOR sends me the questions in advance and I choose carefully, just as I do for the newspaper column. The station has put me in the regular lineup. I'm to start broadcasting on Wednesdays at 4PM. It's not a very popular time slot, but it's a start. "Don't be greedy Hannah," I tell myself.

Saturday's here at last. Of course, I'll be going to visit Tessie, but the joy isn't there like it used to be. We both loved sharing our experiences over mandel bread and a cup of tea in my kitchen. We were never competitive with one another. We cheered when something good happened to the other.

Now, I have to admit, it's depressing to see her. That doesn't mean I am going to stop, not ever. But my role has changed. Now I'm there for support, caring, and loyalty.

Here I am on Bloomfield Street. I ring the bell and Simon answers. He says, "Hannah, I brought Tessie into the parlor for you. She's sitting up. I think maybe she's getting better."

Simon is not facing reality. It's his way of coping. Instead of correcting him, I reply, "Great to hear that, Simon. I can't wait to see her." Why burst his bubble? I'm sure he can't imagine life without Tessie. Frankly, neither can I.

Tessie is sitting on the sofa. Her daughter Alice must have combed her hair this morning and applied perfume and some rouge. We start to chat. I tell Tessie all about the seder, and how proud I was of my kids. Tessie enjoyed hearing Franny's answer to Mrs. Damsky's stuttering theory.

"Your daughter is your defender, Hannah. What could be better?" she asks.

"Her loyalty makes me proud. Teddy loved her comments too. We took his mother down a notch, and I never had to say a word."

Tessie leans close to my ear and whispers, "I want to tell you something. Cousin Richard is always with Irene now. Always. They are holding hands out on the front stoop, very bold if you ask me. Simon and I do not approve. Irish and Jewish? That can't work. Irene's mother Mollie gives them *the look* when she sees them together. But do they care? Those two don't even see the scandal. For them, being together is okay. Oy, what can I do? You always tell me to stay out of people's business, but this? How can I? You have good advice for your letter writers. What about me? Help *me, Hannah.*"

I give it some thought. "With Irene living right next door, I don't see how you can keep them apart. Richard is needy, and Irene is strong and nurturing. It's almost like he counts on her for support. After all, he lost his family in Hungary. He's looking for something or someone to replace that."

Tessie reacts, with anger, "Aren't we enough? I am his older cousin. Where is the respect? We are blood, *mishbuchah*. He can lean on me."

"Well Tessie, you are like a mother figure to Richard. And he may be a little afraid of Simon. Alice has Joe, Alvin is his cute little buddy. But Irene is young and pretty and very interested in Richard. She fills all his needs."

Tessie sits up and says, 'I hope she isn't filling all his needs Hannah. He's too innocent for that."

Tessie stops talking now. She lies back and closes her eyes. I brought some Ponds Lotion. I hope that using it might be soothing and comforting. "Would you like me to give you a little massage? It will get your mind off your concern about Richard."

Tessie nods, half asleep. I gently rub some cream on her face, arms and legs. Alice comes in and helps me. Tessie seems to like the attention. While I rub in the lotion, her daughter massages her scalp and brushes her hair. Then we bring Tessie back to bed. She falls asleep right away. Alice gives me a worried look. What is happening to her mother?

After saying goodbye to the family, I realize that there is something strange going on in that house. I wonder if the Lesters understand what's happening to Tessie. I feel as if sometimes everyone goes on with their lives. They care about her, yes. She was so vibrant. Not anymore. And Simon's comment about her getting better? I think they swing back and forth, from reality to optimism, to not thinking about the illness at all. It might just be the only way to cope. Who am I to judge?

I walk onto the stoop, and, as predicted, Irene and Richard are sitting together. I sit down to join them. Irene says, "Nice to see you again Hannah." She pokes Richard, "*Likewise,*" he says, smiling proudly. Alvin is sitting on the other side of Richard. He has a rope, and is practicing tying and untying knots. "It's for an escape trick, like Harry Houdini," he tells me. Richard gives him a big approving smile. I like seeing Alvin interact with Cousin Richard. It's good for both of them.

Irene continues, "I've been helping Richard learn English. He's doing very well, as you can see. We practice every day. Once he learns, I want to help him apply for a job." Richard looks into Irene's eyes. He appears to worship her. She is a lovely young woman, blond hair which she wears in a short page boy with bangs. She has hazel eyes, and a curvy figure.

I ask, "Do you have a job, Irene?"

"I just finished high school, and there are no jobs right now for me. I've been looking in the classifieds. Someday I want to go to nursing school. Right now, my mother and I take in ironing. It's not much, but it helps," she tells me.

I think for a moment and ask Irene, "Do you think Richard can help Simon with the cleaning business? Maybe his English will improve if he gets out with other people more."

"Richard was an art student before he came to the United States. He has talent, Hannah. I'm sure he could do better than working in a cleaning company," Irene says.

These two are both dreamers, that's clear. I need to ask Richard about his art. Maybe next time he'll show me his work.

The two go back to holding hands. They walk me down the steps to the end of the path, and open the iron gate for me. We wave goodbye. I don't know why, but I have an ominous feeling about those two. Something's up. Tessie may be right after all.

# Recipe for Matzoh Brei

This one is so easy you barely need a recipe. Tastes best the first morning after the Passover Seder. Serve with syrup, jam, apple sauce, sugar, or just plain salt and pepper.

**4 pieces of matzah**
**½ cup water**
**4 eggs**
**Salt and pepper**
**Vegetable oil or butter**

In a large bowl, break medium size pieces of matzah. Add water to cover. Toss the matzah and drain water. Matzah should be moist. Add beaten eggs, salt and pepper. Mix all together with a fork. Over high heat, melt butter or heat up oil in large fry pan. Add mixture and fry until crisp. Turn over, like pancakes.

Serve when browned with your choice of toppings.

# A Family Secret

"Ready to go?" I ask Teddy. It's Thursday afternoon, time to travel to the WOR studios. It's always exciting to go to that part of the city, right near Times Square. I still get butterflies in my stomach as we leave our office. I'm pleased to have Teddy with me for the trip.

"Will I ever get used to this?" I ask.

"I don't think *I'll* ever get used to it, Hannah. Who knew? From a little idea to increase newspaper sales, to a major radio show? It was all your idea, really. I just encouraged you.

"Hannah, think about it. We met each other during a difficult time in our lives, for both of us." Teddy says.

"One door closes and another one opens. I've often heard the expression and now I believe it. I sometimes feel like I'm a character in one of my *Help Me Hannah Letters*," I say with a laugh.

I continue, "Teddy, I want to ask you something that might be uncomfortable for you to answer. Why did you stay single for so long, living with your mother and sisters? It's unusual for a man almost forty. You said scoliosis was the reason. Frankly, I don't believe you."

Teddy takes a deep breath. I've touched a nerve. "Watch out," I tell myself. I may not like the answer.

"I have wanted to talk to you about my past, but I couldn't find the right time. Until now, I've told you only the things that I wanted you to know. But now is not the time. You will need to be clear minded for your show. I want you to know everything. I'll feel better once I get this over with," Teddy tells me, looking down at his hands. We're riding in the subway. Maybe the motion of the train is hypothesizing us a little.

"Let's go back to Goldberg's delicatessen and talk, after the program," I suggest.

My mood has changed and a dark feeling washes over me. Now, in the studio, I go through the sound check, hoping that I'll be able to concentrate on the letters. I must admit, I'm somewhat distracted.

After the introduction, the show begins with this letter, and now I'm fully connected to the program. It's almost a relief. I put all my attention into the task ahead.

I read this letter:

> *I am a 21-year old man. I fell in love with a woman, (I will call her Pearl) who lives on my block. She is a few years older than me. She's 28 and has a little boy. She's always out walking him in his carriage. That's how we met. Whenever we passed on the sidewalk, we both smiled. One day we started talking and became friends.*

*I learned that Pearl's husband left her. He ran off with another woman.*

*I am single, living with my older sister and her husband. Our parents still live in Austria. When I told my sister that I love Pearl, she forbid me to see her. She says I shouldn't be burdened with an older woman and a child who isn't even mine. She threatened to tell my parents. I know they would not approve. My brother-in- law agrees.*

*I love Pearl and I love her son. They need me and I want to help them. I have a good job as a cab driver. I earn enough to support the three of us.*

*Hannah, is it so bad to marry a woman who already has a child? I think my sister is wrong. I want to respect her wishes, after all, she took me into her home. But don't I deserve to be happy and have a family of my own?*

*Signed,*

*Confused*

I pause for just a second, and then respond.

"The fact that Pearl already has a child is a minor problem that can be overcome. And it's possible that you two will have a child of your own together as well. You have a good job and you will be able to support them both. If her ex-husband is truly out of the picture, then I see no reason why you shouldn't marry this woman. Please be sure you truly love her. Don't rush into marriage just because she needs you. But once you know it's right, you should follow your heart.

"If you explain these things, and your plans to your sister, in a calm and sensible way, she might change her mind and come to understand your feelings. Only you can be in control of your life. If you have found true love don't let it slip away."

The *Help Me Hannah* hour flies by. I tried to answer each letter with careful thought and common sense. The staff gives me an approving nod.

Back in the subway Teddy and I are quiet. I can feel him thinking about what he is about to tell me. Once we are seated in Goldberg's, at our favorite table, Teddy orders an egg cream for each of us. No dinner this time. The kids will be waiting for us for supper.

Teddy nervously plays with the salt and pepper shakers on the table. I reach across the table and hold his hand. I force him to look at me. "I want you to be honest. Whatever is bothering you, now is the time to tell me."

Teddy takes a breath. "Hannah, when I was only seventeen, I walked into our apartment after school, to find my father dead. He hanged himself in the bathroom. My mother and sisters were there, but couldn't move him. It was as if they were frozen in shock. I had to take him down and call the police. From that day on, I became the man of the house. It changed me forever.

"You see, Father had a serious mental illness, melancholy, I guess. I'm sure of that now. He had wild mood swings. At times, he would be happy and exuberant. Then sad and depressed. During his depressed periods, he was very distant. He would sit for hours staring into space. At times he wouldn't even speak.

"When he came out of it, he was the fun guy again, he would do crazy things, like spend money he didn't have. Or gamble. He'd stay out late. We wouldn't know where he was. There were times when bill collectors would be at our door. My poor mother was always afraid of losing everything."

It took me a moment to take this information in. Oy, poor Teddy, I thought. "How did you all manage to live? Could a man like that earn a living for his family?" I asked.

"During his good periods, he bought and managed apartment buildings. He lost some of them to gambling debts. Luckily, there was one building that he never lost. That building saved us. I continued to collect the rents, and keep the apartment house in good order. And I still do. We have a good *super*. He's been working for me all these years. That income has allowed me to operate our little newspaper.

But the scars are still with me, Hannah, with all of us. Maybe that's why Mother is the way she is. I think my sisters and I have slowly moved forward. We all lost something along the way. Trust? Faith? Confidence? And the *shonda* of it all was particularly hard on my mother. She was always concerned about how things looked to the neighbors. After the suicide,

215

she cut herself off completely. She rarely leaves home now. Almost never."

"But Teddy, you didn't have friends, dates, parties, clubs? You missed out on so much. How about your physical needs?"

"Let's just say those things can be paid for," Teddy said, looking down again, embarrassed. "I'm sorry, but you should know that, Hannah. I'm not proud, but it's what I did.

"I immersed myself in books. I became self-educated. I went through different phases: science, history, philosophy, politics, Zionism. Reading *The Jewish Daily Forward* was a big part of that. It gave me the idea to start my own small paper, and as you know, it grew from there."

"Teddy, that's one of the things that made me fall in love with you, your intelligence. But why now, do you feel it's okay to be with me, to have me as a friend and then a wife, when it never was okay before to be with other women?" I ask.

"I just knew when we met in Dr. Bader's office that you were the one. I can't explain it," he said, now finally looking right at me. "I think it was timing. It had to be *beshert*. Before you, I questioned my inherited traits. Did mental illness run in my family? If I married and had a child, would that child have the same problems as my father? Would I inherit the problems? Could I be a good father? My insecurities stood in the way. But you already had children. You provided me with an instant family, Hannah. Something I never thought I could have."

We lingered for a while, and then we walked home, arm in arm, with a new sense of closeness. When we walked in the door, the kids greeted us with hugs, Solly shouting, "Mom, I'm starving. I've been practicing my part all afternoon. Wwwwhat's for supper?"

Home sweet home.

# A Celebration

The play, *Tevye The Dairyman* is a big success. We sold tickets to all our family and friends. The play was a Sunday matinee, and I decided to invite some people back to our apartment for a little celebration.

Solly did a fine job, beaming with pride right after the curtain call. When he came out into the audience, we treated him like a movie star, a regular Mickey Rooney.

I had everything set up before we left. My neighbor Claire, who's been so helpful, promised to turn on the coffee pot and help me serve. I made some little sandwiches and cookies. We even served schnapps for the adults, and fruit punch for the kids.

But the favorite delicacy of the night was a large bowl of rice pudding topped with a sprinkle of cinnamon that sat in the middle of the table. I put it in a fancy cut glass bowl on a pedestal. That recipe from Uncle Ben's patient, Mrs. Cappola, is a real winner. Now I know why her family loved it so much. And why Mrs. Cappola wears a size 18.

Alice came with her boyfriend, Joe. She told me that they secretly got engaged. Tessie doesn't know yet. I promised to keep the secret. They came with Richard and Irene, side by side the whole time. Alvin tagged along and congratulated his pal. The two boys are such good buddies. This time Alvin brought a ventriloquist dummy, his latest hobby. That boy has the best imagination. What will he think of next?

It's great to have my Hoboken group here, but without Simon and Tessie, it all feels very strange. My loyal friend wouldn't have missed this party for the world. And she would have had lots to say about all the people the next day. Gossip is a natural pastime for Tessie. Okay, I'll admit it. I enjoy a good story too. Especially with Tessie. Now, it appears, she's too weak to travel here, and Simon would never leave his wife alone.

Franny is talking with Alice, who is a year older. I know Franny looks up to her, almost like a big sister. I notice that limp again. When Franny is tired, the weak leg reappears. Uncle Ben says that she may always have that problem. Franny is a serious girl, strong and outspoken. If she intends to go work on a kibbutz, those traits will surely be helpful.

Teddy's two sisters, Mildred and Evelyn are sitting on the sofa, making small talk with Uncle Ben and Aunt Rose. I love seeing both families showing an interest in each other. Mildred plays piano and is passionate about music. She even loves opera. Evelyn is an avid reader. My uncle and aunt are very cultured. I'm so glad that they have common interests.

The neighborhood kids come wandering in. Once everyone has had a bite to eat, Teddy gets their attention. He raises his glass and says, "Here's to a great performance. Solly did a fine job. I think he loved every minute of it. And so did we. Thank you all for sharing the joy and pride that Hannah and I feel. Let's all raise a glass. *L'Chaim.*"

I watch our friends mingle. It's amazing how many people are able to fit in my small apartment. Tight squeeze. When they all leave, Teddy and I collapse on the sofa. This is the first gathering we've hosted together. I raise my glass and give a private toast. "Here's to us, Teddy." He looks at me with that smile and puts his arm around me.

I almost feel guilty for my happiness. My friend is so ill, and there is nothing I can do to help. My mind goes to a bad place. What will life be like without our little talks, our Saturday visits? Let us have more time together, even if our visits are just a shadow of what they used to be. Tessie still has so much to live for.

# Recipe for Rice Pudding (from Mrs. Cappola)

I love this dessert. It's easy and makes a great impression. Some people like to add raisins, but not me. If you follow my instructions exactly, it should be perfect.

**½ gallon of milk**
**3 large eggs**
**1 cup sugar**
**2 T vanilla**
**1 cup white rice**

Cook rice in milk. Bring to a boil then cook 30-40 minutes until almost all liquid is absorbed.

Mix eggs, sugar, and vanilla together. Beat until foamy. Remove rice from stove. Fold in the mixed ingredients.

Bring to a reboil for one minute. Pour into large glass pan or bowl.

Sprinkle with cinnamon. Refrigerate.

Can be served with whipped cream on top.

# A Thud

Simon called me at seven o'clock this morning. "Tessie is not herself today. She keeps talking about old times, the old days, when she was back in the old country. She seems unhappy. She's living in the past, confused."

"OK, I'll come over, Simon. Maybe seeing me will help."

So, here I am again at 1235 Bloomfield Street. Simon is standing in the doorway. He whispers, "Oy Hannah. I don't know what to do anymore. Every time I try to cheer my Tessie up, she gets angry with me. Nothing helps. Even when I bring her a present. I brought home candy and she wouldn't eat it. Alvin tries too, with his magic tricks. Now he wants to be a ventriloquist. Tessie laughed at that, just a little. Alvin spends all his time trying to make his mother smile."

"Simon, you are a loving husband. You're trying, your children are trying, but the truth is Tessie knows what's happening to her. While you keep the family together, she sees herself as useless. Maybe thinking about the old days helps her to cope. Those were better times. And her memories of life on the farm in Hungary are all the sweeter, compared to these hard times now in the United States."

Simon answers, "I know Hannah, but what if it means she's giving up? She can't give up, Hannah. She can't leave us."

Just then Alice and her boyfriend Joe appear, looking a little uneasy. We greet one another with hugs. Alice gives Joe a little shove. Joe asks, "Um, Mr. Lester? I'd like to talk to you, alone." The two men go into the hallway. They talk softly for a few minutes, and then I hear shouting. Then a loud thud. Then silence. Dead silence.

I go in to see what has happened. Joe is on the ground, not moving. Simon is standing beside him, looking horrified. "No … what have I done?"

Just then, Joe opens his eyes. He slowly stands, exposing a gash on his forehead, blood gushing from the wound. He turns to Alice. "Look what your father did to me."

"Pop," she yells. "Why? Why hurt my Joe like that?"

"I lost my temper Alice. Joe told me he wants to marry you. He asked for my blessing. Is he crazy? You can't go off and get married. Your mother needs you here. We all need you. We can't upset her with this nonsense. She wants you to wait and marry someone worthy of you. With your looks and your brains? Alice please. Mother can't take this news," Simon shouts.

I realize that intervention is needed. "Let's go downstairs into the kitchen. Tessie won't hear us there. Let's talk."

By the time we get downstairs, Alice is crying. I try to console her, with no success. Finally, holding Joe's hand, she tells her father, "You can't stop us Pop. Joe and I *have to* get married. Do you understand or do I have to say the words?"

Silence. Simon is thinking. He may not be the smartest man in the world, but this he can figure out. It's all becoming clear.

Simon sits down, head in his hands. He starts to cry. Alice is sobbing. Poor Joe stands next to Alice, hand on her shoulder. Just then, Simon looks at Joe and says, shaking his fist, red in the face, "What have you done to my daughter, you *mamzer?*"

Joe turns away from Simon and says, "Please Alice, let's leave. We don't need your father's blessing." The two walk out into the street, Alice still sobbing. "And don't come back. You two are *not* welcome here anymore," Simon yells from the front door.

I almost feel embarrassed to have witnessed that encounter. Simon isn't thinking. The family can't survive without Alice and Joe. The cleaning business, care of Tessie? Care of Alvin? Simon could never do it all by himself.

As I walk into Tessie's bedroom, she says, "What was all that noise, Hannah? I heard shouting. Simon's temper again? *Oy gevalt.* What did he do now?"

"Tessie, something has happened. I think Simon should be the one to tell you." Simon overhears and storms into the room. He calls me outside.

225

"I can't upset Tessie. This will kill her, I know it will. She needs to get well and be strong again. I want to keep it a secret."

I answer, "But how can you do that, Simon? Of course, she'll find out. The truth can't be buried. And what about Alvin? He was playing with his toy airplane in your workshop next to the kitchen. I'm sure he heard the shouting."

"Leave it to me, Hannah. I can take care of my family. I have to do this my way. I can't believe that *mamzer* got my daughter pregnant. Tessie must never know."

I say, "Okay, Simon. Do what you think is best." As I walk out the front door, and down the street, I spot Alice. She had been waiting for me.

"Joe and I are going to stay with his parents until things settle down. Joe is furious about the fight and the nasty names. But I know my father. He'll get over this. It may take some time. I'll go into the house when Pop is working and talk to Mom. Yes, she'll be mad. But I know she loves me. She'll forgive me."

"I agree with you Alice. You're her daughter. You have always been a loyal, wonderful girl. These things happen. You and Joe love one another. This is not the first time a baby is conceived before marriage. It would be wise to get married soon."

I leave Hoboken with a heavy heart.

# Help Me Hannah #14

Hannah,

I married a much older man who is a widower with two grown children. He is an educated businessman of means. I was his secretary. We have a good life together. Except for one thing.

His children are very rude to me. Clearly, they don't like me, at all. My husband is distressed about it, and he knows it's upsetting to me. We are not with them very often, but when we are, for holidays or family gatherings, they ignore me.

Do you think they are jealous? Are they worried about their inheritance? I want to talk to them about it, but my husband says no. Should I say anything, or just feel bad. I am torn.

Signed,

Confused

· · · · · · ·

Dear Confused,

This is a common problem. There are really no good solutions. His children should be happy that their father is not alone. But they are selfish. Your suspicion about jealousy and money are probably correct. It is to be expected.

*In my opinion, only your husband can set them straight. He needs to talk to his children about their behavior towards you. If he does, and the rudeness continues, I suggest that you hold your head high, be cordial when you must, but have little to do with them. You must accept this fate and move on. Focus on your good marriage and be grateful for that.*

# Opportunities

It's been two weeks since the incident on Bloomfield Street. Teddy and I are in the kitchen finishing up our supper. I made one of Teddy's favorite dishes, liver and onions. With more money coming in now, we can afford to eat better cuts of meat. But liver is always a treat for us. Maybe it's sentimental. Who knows?

The children have finished eating and are listening to Abbott and Costello on the radio in the parlor. I love these times when it's just the two of us at the kitchen table together, drinking our tea.

Teddy asks me how things are going with the Lester family. I look up from my cup. "Tessie has learned about the pregnancy and to the surprise of her family, she handled the news pretty well. Simon, on the other hand, is still furious. He's been working with Joe, but they don't speak to each other. Alice arranges the schedule so that they have minimum contact. A small private marriage ceremony was performed with only the parents of the bride and groom and the rabbi. It was on Bloomfield Street so that Tessie could be there. Simon attended but didn't say a word. Evidently, he was stone-faced the whole time, according to Tessie. The young couple now lives in a small apartment above Joe's parents' toy store.

And Cousin Richard has been helping Simon. He's pretty good at cleaning and polishing. Irene has offered to help with Tessie's care, now that Alice has moved out. I think Irene likes tending to Tessie's needs. After all, now she gets to be closer to Richard."

Teddy thinks about all this, pauses and says, "Well Hannah, that's a lot for one family to handle. I hope they will get through without too much pain.

"Now I have some interesting news for you," Teddy continues. "WOR contacted me at the paper yesterday. They want a meeting with you and me."

I hold my breath. I've been waiting for something more to happen. I'm very aware that the *Help Me Hannah* radio show is gaining in popularity. Letters have been pouring in. "What do you think Teddy? It's got to be something good."

"Slow down lady. Don't count your chickens. Let's see what they have to say. The gentleman who contacted me is a Mr. Fred Green, Director of Programming for the radio station. We have an appointment after the show airs on Thursday," Teddy responds, always the clear-headed realist.

Together we take the dishes off the table, to the sink. I wash and Teddy dries. Abe never did that, and I appreciate Teddy's helpful ways. We talk some more about the possibilities with WOR. Then Teddy joins the kids in the parlor and I decide to run a hot bath for myself.

As I get into the tub, I add some bath salts, and step in, one foot at a time. The water's hot, just the way I like it. I'm glad the children are listening to their shows with Teddy. I love to hear their laughter. He has become a wonderful figure in their lives. It's his easy temperament. He doesn't try to control them or to be a father to them. I know the father part will come in time.

As I sink into the soothing water and try to imagine what the WOR meeting might be like. I try to think what my part of the conversation might be. I want to tell Mr. Green my theories on the program's success. Why did I love to read *A Bintel Brief* in *The Jewish Daily Forward*? They were my solace after Abe died. And why do my listeners faithfully tune in each Wednesday?

I know that for me, reading and hearing about the problems of others is a wonderful way to distract from *my* worries. After all, my problems seem minor in comparison. And that is the secret to my success. My program allows people to escape their own concerns, even their own miseries. As I rehearse this explanation, I gain confidence.

I get out of the tub, use my Ponds skin cream on my arms and legs. I give my hair one hundred brush strokes. Franny is in her room, reading, of course. Solly's fast asleep. Teddy and I have the night to ourselves. If I were to give myself advice right now, it would be to enjoy this moment. I take a deep breath and put on my new silk nightgown, and dab a little *Evening in Paris* on the warm parts of my body. The night is just beginning.

# Recipe for Hannah's Liver and Onions

We love liver and onions in my house. It's easy to make and always tasty. The more onions the better.

**1 lb. calf's liver**
**2 onions**
**1 T of oil or chicken fat**
**Salt and Pepper**

Cut 1 pound of calf's liver into bite size pieces. Set aside.

Sauté 2 onions in oil in frying pan until golden brown. Then, add liver, seasoned with salt and pepper.

Cook for about 10 minutes.

Now, remove from stove and leave pot covered until liver is cooked throughout.

# Full Time

"Teddy, help me decide which outfit to wear for the WOR meeting," I yell from the bedroom. I'm all jitters today. Better calm down. I settle upon my new cream-colored V neck blouse. It fits perfectly, and I tuck it into my burgundy skirt. My trusty pearls save the day. They brighten up my face and they add a touch of class. I learned that trick from Aunt Rose. I put on pumps with a medium size heel. A quick look in the mirror, check that stocking seams are straight, and off we go. Teddy never has a chance to give me his opinion, although the smile on his face indicates approval.

We're at the WOR studios. The broadcast went smoothly today. My letter choices were of broad interest. As promised, Mr. Green leads us into his office for our meeting. He begins by congratulating me on a great program.

"You have a knack for presenting interesting letters, Hannah. Our listeners have responded with enthusiasm. Ratings are way up, and the ad men are selling commercials for a prime amount of money. What is your secret Hannah?"

"Thank you, Mr. Green. I believe that people love to hear about the problems of others. Hardship teaches us how to live. We can all learn how to navigate our own lives this way. And let's face it, the problems of others make us forget our own worries. I believe that's my secret," I pause, smile, and look directly into his eyes.

"Do you think you would have enough material for a daily program. Monday through Friday? Every week? WOR would like to change our programming schedule to fit you in daily."

This is even better than I expected, I think while trying to look calm. "I'm willing to consider your offer Mr. Green. It's very exciting. It will take me some time to gather enough material, and to create an expanded format for the show. I hope you and my husband, Mr. Damsky, will work out the salary structure and legal details. Business matters aren't my area of expertise."

The men begin talking, and I pretend to pay attention. I have perfect trust in Teddy. He's proven himself to be a savvy money manager. In the meantime, I struggle to contain my composure. I want to make the program unique. I will elaborate on each letter. I will study psychology. I will add more explanation for each problem. I might invite guest experts to the program. Oh, the possibilities are endless.

When the meeting ends, Teddy and I stop at Horn and Hardart again. We're becoming regulars. Teddy begins, "Well Hannah, you have hit the jackpot. WOR is offering you $40 a week, plus a bonus which will depend on advertisers. You will be expected to promote yourself with

Women's Clubs, Church and Synagogue groups, even placing articles in women's magazines. Your show will be a half hour, five days a week, Hannah. This is a full-time job and more. Are you ready for it?"

After hearing his words, my answer is, "I can't do it alone. You've been my unofficial manager and agent. If I'm to do all that Mr. Green has asked of me, would you be willing to work full-time on this venture, as my partner Teddy?"

"How will I run *The Jewish Gazette* and work on *Help Me Hannah*? God willing, the possibilities are incredible for you, and for us. We can't let this go. Let me see if my Assistant Editor would like to take over. We can restructure, or find someone to buy us out. It won't be the first time I take a chance, Hannah." Teddy takes my hand in his.

When we get home, Teddy and I go into the parlor, arms around each other. There's so much work to do. Planning, organizing, structuring the show. We talk for a few moments, and then I put my head on Teddy's shoulder. He gently lifts my hair and kisses my neck. I never get tired of Teddy's affection.

Very early the next morning, while the children are still asleep, I find an envelope on the kitchen table. It says *Help Me Hannah* on the front. The handwriting looks suspiciously like Franny's. I tear it open and start to read.

*Dear Mom,*

*You help so many people. Now I need you to help me. You know how much I have wanted to go to Eretz Y'Israel. I have never stopped dreaming of my life there, ever since I met Mrs. Meir. Now I have the opportunity.*

*My Youth Group is raising money for a movement called Youth Aliyah. Henrietta Szold is our founder. I have applied to work on a new kibbutz called Ein Harod in the Jezreel Valley. There are funds that will cover my transportation. Many important Jews believe that we are doing a smart thing. Even Eddie Cantor is subsidizing the cause. Our plan is to resettle Jewish children from France and other countries in Europe. They need help to escape from persecution. I truly believe that we will save lives.*

*Mother, I am afraid to talk to you in person because I know you think I'm too young. I have graduated from High School, as you wanted. Now I must go.*

*I hope you understand that I'm not like the other girls. I don't care about getting married and having children. That life doesn't appeal to me. It never did and it never will. I want to be a person of substance.*

*I know you help your other letter writers, why not help me? Please give me permission to follow my heart.*

*Your loving daughter,*

*Frances*

I slowly take out my pen and paper. Then the words come easily.

*To my dear daughter,*

*I have given your request a lot of thought. Of course, as a mother, I am fearful of the unknown. You are a serious young lady, smart and caring. True, you are not like the other girls. You were meant to do important things, and I admire your determination.*

*I hope that your courage will boost my courage. Although I will worry about you, I give you permission to follow your heart and your dream.*

*You must promise that you will write and let me know, always, that you are safe.*

*Your loving Mother*

I tiptoe into the bedroom and put my reply on Franny's pillow, careful not to wake her. There will be plenty of time to talk about her travels when she wakes up. For now, sleep peacefully my beautiful brave daughter.

*Barbara Pressman*

# A Glimmer of Hope

It's been a week since the WOR offer. Teddy and I have been working non-stop on the *Help Me Hannah* radio broadcasts and the speaking engagements that we had promised. We both feel confident that we can do this. If I work on the letters and my answers, Teddy says he can handle the other aspects, business, contracts, travel, publicity.

And then there's my Franny. I'm reluctantly letting her go. When she read my response to her letter, she hugged me and said, "Mom, thanks for giving me permission, but I was going anyway. Nothing can stop me."

"Darling, just promise me you'll be careful and write often," I say, forcing myself to smile. I can't let my worry affect her. I need to find a way in my own mind and heart to accept this *new* daughter of mine. This is not the life I imagined for her. But that's my problem, not hers.

It's Saturday, and I'm getting ready for my usual visit to Tessie.

When I arrive in Hoboken, I walk up the steps of the brownstone, and see Irene sweeping the front porch. Richard is polishing the brass doorknob. Aha, progress. At least they're not sitting on the stoop making eyes at each other. We exchange warm greetings, and I knock on the front door. I can't contain my excitement, so much news this week to tell Tessie.

Alvin opens the door, and gives me a hug. "You are getting taller everyday Alvin," I say, although Alvin is very small for his age. I give him a piece of peppermint candy from my purse and his eyes light up.

"Mom is waiting for you in the kitchen," he says. "She's sitting at the table." he says, all happy and bright eyed.

"Good morning, *mein* Hannah. I have something to tell you. Sit," she says, patting the chair next to her. I'm thinking "This is a different Tessie."

"Your uncle told me that a special doctor wants to help me with my brain disease. He works with radiation. Dr. Bader wants me to try."

"That's wonderful news Tessie. Looks like you feel better just thinking about it." Alvin stands by, beaming. To myself, I wonder. Radiation can be harsh. I've heard a little about it. If Uncle Ben thinks it's a good idea, then it must be. Meanwhile, let Tessie dream of her cure.

"I want to get better for my family, Hannah. They all need me. And a new grandchild? Oy, that baby. I'm going to need to teach Alice how to care for a child. I pray for a beautiful baby girl, with curly hair and blue eyes. I can picture her in

240

my mind, God willing." We both smile dreamily. "Let's not give it a *kinehora,*" we both say simultaneously.

Tessie sighs, "If only I could get Simon to understand and forgive. He loves his Alice. But Joe? He wants to kill him. I can't believe they work together without speaking. *Oy gevalt,* I'm glad I don't have to see that, day after day. I'm hoping that once the baby comes, Simon will change his mind."

"I hope you're right. But now it's my turn, Tessie. You won't believe my news." I give her the WOR story first.

"Hannah. I always knew you could do it. You are going to a rich lady, my friend. *Mazel Tov.* I hope you won't get too big for your britches. Don't forget where you came from. And don't ever forget your old friend from Hoboken. Alvin, please get me some of Pop's wine and two glasses. We need to celebrate this one."

"Drink during the day? Oh, why not? We have so much to be thankful about," I laugh. "And there's more Tessie. Franny is going to go work on a kibbutz, near Jerusalem. Remember how she was so fascinated by Golda's lectures? Well, she is going to help continue that work."

"Oy Hannah, is that safe?"

I try to sound sure about it. Tessie notices a little tremor in my voice. She attempts to reassure me, "Sometimes we have to take a chance. Look, I came here from Hungary on a boat when I was even younger than Franny. My parents forbid me and I came anyway, against their wishes. I snuck away. I always had too much *chutzpah* for my own good, a regular *bonditt*," Tessie says. We pause to take a sip of Simon's homemade wine. It feels warm and sweet going down. Mmmmm, perfect.

Tessie continues, "Look, my Alice doesn't live with me anymore. What can you do? Kids move on. Suddenly, Tessie looks exhausted. Oh Hannah, I want to get back in bed. This has been a lot of excitement for me today. You and Alvin better walk me to the bedroom." It's as if the energetic new *Tessie balloon* has deflated. My heart sinks. Was this just a temporary moment of hope?

After we get Tessie settled in her bed, blanket over her frail body, pillow fluffed, eyes closed, I say a gentle, contented goodbye and tiptoe out the door. This was a nice visit. There is some hope for Tessie's future. It's a small glimmer of hope, but hope is a powerful thing.

While riding the trolley to the ferry, I think about my next *Help Me Hannah* letter. I can't wait to get home, sit down and get started. I received this one yesterday. I think it will be perfect.

# Help Me Hannah # 15

*Dear Hannah,*

*I just graduated from George Washington High School, with honors. I've always been a good student and a good girl. I love to read and learn new things. I am the editor of my school newspaper.*

*My dream has been to go to Hunter College and become an English teacher. I have been accepted there already.*

*I am an only child. My father left my mother and me when I was 5-years old. He comes into our lives, then leaves. This is his pattern. Sometimes he asks my mother if he can borrow money. She always says yes. Then he leaves and never pays it back.*

*My mother works hard doing piece work. She sews for a coat factory. She only makes $10 a week.*

*Because of my mother's small income, I can't afford to go to Hunter College. I have an opportunity to work in a dentist's office. My mother wants me to take the job. But it's not my dream. Will I ever be able to be a teacher? My heart is broken.*

*Signed,*

*A disappointed scholar*

• • • • • • •

*Dear Scholar,*

*You sound like an intelligent and hard-working person. Your mother is right. You must take the job. These days, no one can turn down steady income. Why don't you register for Hunter or City College, part-time, at night? Tuition is free. It will take longer to finish, but you can earn your degree and fulfill your dream.*

*I predict you will succeed. Hard work and patience never hurt anyone.*

# Part 5: Nothing Stays the Same

## More Space

A year has passed. Tessie is doing quite well. The treatments seem to have slowed the growth of her brain tumor. We are all encouraged.

Teddy seems uneasy this evening. "Hannah, I need to pay a visit to my mother on Sunday. I'm hoping you will come with me this time," Teddy asks. I can hear the unease in his voice. We've just finished supper. Things have not gone well with Teddy's mother since my radio show has taken off. It has affected our marriage.

*Help Me Hannah*, on WOR, has become quite a popular series. My time slot is 10 AM Monday through Friday. The expanded listening audience has made me a household name for women in the New York area. We have wonderful advertisers now. Ivory Snow, Kellogg's Cereal, and Frigidaire to name a few. Teddy is now on the payroll, devoting his time exclusively to producing the program.

We've moved to a larger apartment. We need a home office and more room to entertain guests. As you can see, our lives have changed. It's all very exciting. Teddy and I still pinch ourselves.

Mrs. Damsky, my *dear* mother-in-law on the other hand, is not too pleased. Her darling son Teddy is no longer available to nurture her selfish needs. Any attention away from her becomes a threat, in her mind. That threat, of course, is me. Although Teddy has broken away, I know he feels guilty. Mrs. Damsky insinuates, not too subtly, that we are becoming snobs.

Teddy gets little reminders weekly about his obligations. He is still her handyman, money provider, and emotional support. He shouldn't think that he's some *uppity radio man*. As you can imagine, he usually visits his mother without me. I find it's better that way.

"I'm all yours for Sunday," I say, trying to sound cheerful. Teddy's been so good to me, the least I can do is support him when he visits. It may seem like I'm a *diva* now, a radio personality and all. But I hope I haven't lost my values. Tessie reminds me of this all the time.

Sunday has arrived. After breakfast, I go to Wolf's Bakery on the corner. I don't want to walk in empty-handed. Teddy asks, "Are you almost ready, Hannah? Let's go over there early today. I need to pay the bills, fix the wobbly leg on the dining room table, and spend some time visiting with my mother and sisters. Evelyn said they are preparing lunch for us. Let's try to patch things up."

"I promise I'll try. I don't have much hope. Your mom can't get past our success. She wants you to be totally devoted to her needs. You should have no other life but that. And I think she wishes that you and I never met, Teddy."

"Please understand what she's been through Hannah. It has been hard for her after my father's suicide. I've been her lifeline, a replacement husband. She can't lose me. In her mind, she constantly worries that I'll forget her now that I have you," Teddy says in a pleading voice.

I sigh and respond, "I'll give it my best Teddy. Solly will join us. He can be our little distraction."

We walk in and kiss hello, like usual. Solly shows the sisters his newest card trick. Mildred pretends to be dazzled and says, "*Mein zissen boychik*, you fooled me again. How do you do it every time?"

Solly blushes and says, "I've also been memorizing a poem to recite for school. I've chosen *Casey at the Bat*. Would you like to hear it?"

"Sure," they nod enthusiastically and Solly begins his recitation, without a stutter or stammer. We all clap and Solly takes a bow. My little performer.

Mrs. Damsky, (I still call her that) remains seated in the kitchen. I can't bring myself to call her Mom and she hasn't asked me to either. Teddy and I walk in. I present my bakery box of cookies. "What happened? Did you forget how to bake?"

Teddy says, "Come on Mom, give Hannah a break. That comment was uncalled for. Hannah works so many hours now. Things have changed for her."

"Sure, take her side. What kind of son does that? *Oy, mein heart*," she cries, gasping for breath.

I'm thinking, *A regular Sarah Bernhardt. Who could fall for this?* But the look on Teddy's face tells me that someone has fallen for it. He looks absolutely crushed. My Teddy is a fine man and this woman takes advantage of his good nature.

"Come Mrs. Damsky. Why don't you and I have a little talk while Teddy works on that wobbly table? Tell me how you've been feeling this week." I know talking about her health is a favorite topic.

She groans, "Nice of you to ask Hannah. You're usually too busy helping strangers. Well, my hip hurts when I wake up in the morning. I can hardly get out of bed. And if I exert myself, my heart beats too fast. I'm worried sometimes about a broken heart with all the disappointments I've had in my life."

*Okay Mrs. Damsky*, I think to myself. *She has opened up to me. Now this I can deal with. Be the good listener that you are Hannah. Let her talk.*

"I imagine that must be hard, Mrs. Damsky. Teddy has told me just a little bit about your life's disappointments. He respects your privacy. But look, we're family now."

My mother- in-law lets down her guard, just a little. "That's true Hannah. When my husband died, my life ended. All I ever do is sit at home. I hardly ever leave the house. I'm so ashamed of what happened. I hate knowing that people feel sorry for me. They used to look, and point. Who needs those *yentas* in my building whispering about that horrible day?

"Oy, but at least I still have my daughters. Now, of course, Teddy is gone, thanks to you."

I reply, "Teddy loves you very much. He is not gone, will never be gone. You raised a fine man, Mrs. Damsky. I respect his loyalty to you. I hope you know that." With those words, I gently put my hands on hers, and then give them a squeeze. I look right into her eyes. Surprisingly, she doesn't move away.

"Well you two are fancy people now, in your new big fancy apartment house. With your fancy new furniture and fancy new friends. Where do I fit in?"

"A man always needs his mother. Teddy counts on your love, Mrs. Damsky. I think he genuinely enjoys helping you."

"Well I need his help Hannah. More than you do. You're still a young woman, with your whole life ahead of you. Look at me. Where do I fit in with your new rich friends? I'm not part of Teddy's life anymore. I'm just a burden these days."

"No more feeling sorry for yourself, Mrs. Damsky. We are family. Please get used to that fact. I have your best interests at heart, just like Teddy does."

My mother-in-law gives a little snicker, then a sigh of resignation. I feel as if I might have gotten through to her this time.

We all have a nice lunch after Teddy fixes the dining room table. Solly seems to bask in the attention of his female audience. We eat the store-bought cookies for dessert and say our goodbyes. Mrs. Damsky embraces her son, then everyone gives my Solly a kiss. My mother-in-law shyly reaches out to me as well. This is a first. I hug her back. Teddy is beaming.

On the way home, Teddy says, "Hannah, you've worked your magic. What did you say to Mother in the kitchen?"

"I listened to her concerns and reassured her that I would never take you away. I think we made some history today Teddy," I laugh. Even Solly gives a chuckle. Teddy holds me close. I know how important this was for him.

After we get home I find some time to get back to one of my favorite pastimes, reading. To escape from the pressures of my job, I've been reading *Gone with the Wind*. It's all the rage these days. It's a very long book, taking me forever to finish. The independence of Scarlet O'Hara inspires me. I've been trying to keep up with the literary world now. I need to broaden myself in this new role of mine. We are hoping to interview celebrities and authors on the radio show. But that's somewhere in the future.

Sometimes I stop and think how lucky I am to live in the United States, where we can read anything we like. Right now, in Europe they've been burning books. Germany has become a dangerous place. I once heard a saying, *Where ever they burn books, they will eventually burn human beings.* That scares me.

True to her word, Franny has been sending letters. They are my lifeline to my precious daughter. Franny can't tell me everything that she's doing. Some if it is secret work. Reading between the lines, I sense it.

*Dear Mother,*

*Please don't worry about me. I am as happy as I have ever been in my life. My fellow halutzim and I have been working very hard. We consider ourselves pioneers. The farming is not easy. There are chickens to feed, fields to plow, and fruits and vegetables to harvest. But Mother, I have never tasted such delicious flavors, especially our oranges. Everything we eat is fresh and healthy. We are outside all day, working collectively. I like the fact that there is no private property. We don't even receive wages. Men and women are equals. I just love that.*

*I've been making even more new friends. Lots of them are from Poland, because Zionism is very strong there. And some are from Russia, Germany, Hungary, even South Africa. One new friend told me about a pogrom in his Russian village. He said he saw a little boy shot right in front of his parents. But we can't dwell on the sadness. Those tragedies only make us stronger. We must stay positive and work toward our goals.*

*Last night we danced the Hora in a big circle. My heart beat quickly as the music got faster. We were all spinning around until we felt dizzy. Oh, what a glorious night.*

*Mother, we also have our problems. Our Arab neighbors have not welcomed us. There is disease in the region as well. The British try to keep the peace. We have our own strong security, so we feel safe.*

*Please tell Solly that I miss him. He is always in my heart. I hope that Solly has been putting coins in the JNF box. We need those donations desperately to plant trees and buy land. We kibbutzniks can't do it alone.*

*Oh, and Mother, I almost forgot to tell you how proud I am of you and your program, Help Me Hannah. The new apartment sounds beautiful. I miss you all.*

*Goodbye for now.*

*Your loving daughter Frances*

# Bathtub Boat

Tessie continues taking her radiation treatments. They are experimental and appear to be helping, at least for now. She's lost some of her ability to speak and think clearly. She forgets a lot. But the one thing she did not lose was hope. Powerful, life affirming hope. Tessie, the fighter, has hope. At times she is as clear as a bell, insightful, feisty, honest. She makes us think the old Tessie has returned. And then she crashes.

"Good morning, merry sunshine," I call out as I enter her bedroom. I brought some sweet potatoes from the sweet potato man's pushcart, hot and steamy for her and for Alvin to eat. I know he loves them.

Tessie responds, "Good Morning, mein famous radio star. Thanks for remembering your old best friend. I'm honored. Help me prop up this pillow. Oy, I can never get comfortable lately."

"Hannah, do you think Simon will be able to take Alvin shopping for his Bar Mitzvah suit? We have to prepare. Alvin needs to be ready by May. Simon says he knows how to drive a bargain. Oy, if I could only go to help. With Simon and his temper, I just don't know."

I think for a minute and reply, "It's very important for Simon to buy his only son a Bar Mitzvah suit. Those two need more togetherness. Tessie, you need to show Simon that you trust him. Let him go with Alvin to the Lower East Side."

"Hannah, I hope you're right, but I'm not so sure. Will you stay a while today? Alice is coming by to drop off some food for us. She's bringing little Ruth. Oy that child, you could just squeeze that *punim* of hers. And her gorgeous curls Hannah, just like mine but light brown. A regular Shirley Temple.

"Joe won't be here though. He prefers to stay away from Simon, even though they've been working pretty well together. Simon is still cold as ice to him. I wish he would let it go already," Tessie says, eyes downward.

I'm sure this rift must be awful for the whole family. Alice is still the apple of Simon's eye. Ruthie is a close second.

"I do have time today Tessie. But let me go right now to see Alvin. You rest up."

I give Alvin his sweet potato treat. He thanks me but looked dejected.

"What's wrong my sweetheart?" I ask as I bend to his eye level.

"I'll show you," he states solemnly as he takes my hand and leads me to the bathroom, pointing to the bathtub.

There is a copy of *Modern Mechanics* magazine on the floor, next to the tub, open to a page of directions. Inside the tub filled with water, is a sad looking version of an Ironclad Civil War Battleship, listing on its side. It consists of a cheese box, a food can and a spool from thread. The spool is supposed to be the cannon, Alvin explains. "Pop and I worked together on this. We followed the directions exactly. Pop can fix anything. He can build anything. But look at my battleship. It can't even stay afloat," he said, wiping his tears away.

I give him a hug. What else can I do? As I walk into the hallway, I see Simon. He must have overheard. He walks into the bathroom and says, "Stop crying Alvin. Be a man," and storms out to the front stoop.

Better leave this problem alone. I go back to Tessie but I don't tell her about the bathtub boat incident. Frankly, I'm so pleased that she's doing this well. Today. Why give her anything to ruin this mood.

Alice and the baby have just arrived. What a commotion. Tessie gazes at little Ruthie, Alvin runs in and lifts her into Tessie arms. Now I know why Tessie has a will to live.

I stay a little longer. What a beautiful scene. I absorb it all, fearful that these happy times won't last forever. Then I decide to let this precious family unit enjoy their very special moment.

Off to the trolley, the ferry, then home at last. *I can't wait to see my very own precious ones,* I think to myself.

Afterwards, I get ready for next week's radio show by searching through the letters on my desk in my new, spacious, wonderful home office.

# Help Me Hannah # 16

*Dear Hannah,*

*I am a man of 70 years. I have a good wife, one grown son, and a nice apartment in the Bronx. As I get older, I think more and more about my old life in Czechoslovakia and the family I left behind before coming to America.*

*One incident has been haunting me with guilt. I cannot let it go. My father was a horseman. Everyone in our little village knew of his skill. One day, my father was bringing his white fury back to the barn. The horse had other ideas. It reared back on its hind legs, hitting the rear wall of the stall. One of the iron shod front hooves found my father's head, struck his temple, and he went down, hard.*

*My father lay in bed for a week, swollen, and puffy, drifting in and out of consciousness. Each night, Father would whisper to me to fix him a baked potato, put it in a crock and mix it with sour cream and buttermilk. It was his favorite forbidden delicacy. I did this for three nights. I watched him eat it with great satisfaction. After the third night, he fell into a deep and fitful sleep. I never told my mother about the potatoes. He never recovered, and died just a few days later.*

*I wonder, did I contribute to his death? Please Hannah, help me with my guilt and grief, all these years later.*

*Sincerely,*

*A guilty son*

• • • • • • •

*Dear Guilty Son,*

*You must have loved your father very much. Of course, you did <u>not</u> contribute to his death. His horse was responsible for that. He loved and trusted you enough to keep his little secret. You enabled him to have moments of joy before dying. You sent him to his final sleep with a good taste in his mouth. That was a gift.*

# Bar Mitzvah Suit

As soon as I walk into the house on 1235 Bloomfield Street for my weekly visit, Tessie says, "Well, my fancy friend, you were right this time. That's why you are a respected advice giver on the radio," Tessie tells me. "Simon finally did a good thing Hannah. He bought Alvin a suit fit for a king. And what a price. He outsmarted those *gonnifs* on the Lower East Side. Then she yells, "Simon, bring the suit in here so Hannah can see the craftsmanship."

Simon proudly carries the suit in like he's carrying a trophy. His blue eyes light up as he starts to tell me his story:

"Hannah," he says softly, "I told Tessie I know how to do these things, but she never believes me. I can be a very good businessman. Well, now she finally believes me." Simon, beaming, then relates his 'suit buying triumph' to me.

"First, I taught Alvin all about the tricks we would use to get the best price. He must never let on that he likes the clothes. We made a signal, two pulls on my coat if he likes the suit. That was the first part of our plan.

"Next, when we arrived on Orchard Street, we strolled by the window of Marcus and Feingold, examining the mannequins, but not going in, of course. You never want to look too interested, you see. We silently made our choice, but we didn't let on. Soon, Marcus comes outside and invites us into the shop. He shows us a new line of suits, so fancy that they have pleated pockets, all the rage in Paris, he tells us. Marcus says, 'Feel this cloth. The finest on Orchard Street. You don't have to buy. Just try on the jacket for size,' he says. 'In fact, Feingold was saving this very suit for his own son's Bar Mitzvah. But he's out to lunch right now. Ah, this suit was made for your beautiful *boychik*. It's a steal for 25 dollars.'

"Then Hannah, I told him that just because I come from Jersey doesn't mean I don't know cheesecloth from gabardine. I'm not doing business with a *gonnif*. That's way too much money. Marcus says to me, 'Where else can you get four pieces: knickers, vest, long pants and a jacket for that kind of money? Go back to New Jersey where you belong.'

"I grab Alvin's hand and we march out the door. Alvin's crying already because he really wants the suit. I whisper he should be patient. We go away and buy some half sour pickles, some lox, some herring, wrapped in paper. We killed some time. Then, we slowly walk past the store again, not even looking in the window. Marcus sees us and comes running out. 'So, I see you didn't buy a suit?'

"I tell him I can't buy a suit. I spent so much money on all this food. Now, I only have 15 dollars left in my pocket. Marcus tells me he wouldn't want this fine young boy to go home empty handed. 'I'll tell you what. You can have the suit for fifteen dollars. Feingold may kill me, but the suit is yours.'"

Simon walks out of the bedroom, beaming. I've never known Simon to talk this much in all the years I've known him.

When Simon is out of hearing range, Tessie whispers to me, "Of course, Simon spent more on the suit than he makes in a week. And the suit is too big for Alvin, but Alice and I can fix that. After all, a deal is a deal," she laughs, with great delight.

I leave Hoboken today with a lighter step.

# Help Me Hannah # 17

*Dear Help Me Hannah,*

*I am an immigrant and have lived in New York for five years. I work on the docks, loading and unloading cargo. All day I lift heavy things. I sweat a lot. I come home, shower, eat and go to bed.*

*One day I saw an ad in the newspaper for dance lessons at Arthur Murray Studios. I cleaned myself up after work and signed up for lessons. Kathryn Murray was my teacher. When she would demonstrate a new step, she chose me as her partner.*

*I surprised myself. I was a natural. I have rhythm and am quite graceful. Many women wanted to be my partner.*

*But one in particular kept looking at me. So, I asked her to dance. Our bodies fit and we moved like one. She is always smiling when she looks at me. She is very pretty, and American born. She doesn't even have an accent. She speaks as well as Eleanor Roosevelt.*

*I want to ask her for a date. But I am not worthy of her social standing. What's the point? I'm afraid she will laugh at me.*

*Do I have a chance, Hannah? What should I do?*

*Signed,*

*Insecure*

· · · · · · ·

*Dear Insecure,*

*Why do you believe you are not worthy of this young lady? You say she smiles at you and you dance well together.*

*Think about it this way. If she doesn't want your company, she will say no. It may sting at first, but that's all. It will be over and you will have your answer. You will never know unless you try.*

*If she says yes, then you have a chance for a future with her. Right now, think only about one date at a time. You can ask her out for coffee after the dance class. Go slowly, be brave and let your heart lead the way.*

# A Portrait

"Hannah, come see what Cousin Richard has made for me, in honor of Alvin's Bar Mitzvah."

And there it is, standing on an easel that Simon made, an original portrait of Alvin in his Bar Mitzvah suit. A perfect likeness. Even those bright blue eyes. Who knew Richard was so talented? I guess Irene did. We didn't believe her.

Tessie says, "Each time I look at it I remember that glorious day, Hannah. And to think that I was actually able to go to shul, even though I needed lots of help. At least I was there. That was my desire. Just to be there."

"Alvin did a fine job Tessie. OK, so what if he had to stand on a soap box to be seen," I say. We both laugh. "The kiddish was perfect too. Simon's wine was a big hit. And I was proud to serve my mandel bread."

"As usual," Tessie says. "I was proud that you were there, my big shot friend. Teddy was proud to have you on his arm, anyone could see that. Even little Ruthie cooperated, sleeping through most of the service."

The Bar Mitzvah seems to have brought the Lester family together, partly because of Simon's newly found confidence in his negotiating abilities. Tessie has been going easy on him these days. He doesn't lose his temper as long as Tessie doesn't hurt his feelings, it seems. Maybe she realizes that Simon will need to be a calm, head of the household one day soon. Who knows when? But we all sense that it's coming. I know Tessie senses it too.

I make my visit a short one today. So much work to do at home. I find that there aren't enough hours to read through my mail, prepare for speaking engagements, and, of course, keep up with my family life. I will never stop making my family come first.

I find Richard sitting on the stoop with Irene when I leave. "You really are talented Richard. The portrait of Alvin is wonderful," I tell him.

He blushes and thanks me. "I want to make more," he says, Irene beaming by his side.

"Have you ever painted murals Richard?"

He nods his head. "Yes, in art school in Budapest."

Irene jumps in, "I just know Richard can make something of himself in this country with his artwork Hannah."

Then I get an idea. "Irene, what if you and Richard talk to some bar owners about Richard's art and suggest that he can paint a mural for them? Many taverns have beautiful city scenes. You will need to speak for him Irene, until his English improves."

Irene's eyes light up. "I would be happy to do that Hannah. Richard and I can go together. We will bring some examples of his work. I could help Richard with his murals too, if that would be alright with you, Richard," she says. Richard nods his head, blushing once again.

These two are going to be OK. Besides her friendship with Richard, Irene has been a great help with Tessie in Alice's absence. And she nurtures Richard like a boy who's lost his family, which he has. The Lesters have welcomed Irene as one of their own. Funny how things work out sometimes.

At home, I sit in my office chair and admire my beautiful new walnut writing desk. It has lots of drawers and small compartments. The panel that folds down is very roomy for reading and writing my *Help Me Hannah* letters. As I start working on the next letter, Teddy walks in. His desk is on the other side of the office. We often work together. I marvel at how he handles all the appointments and money matters, while still keeping a hand in *The Jewish Gazette*. Luckily his assistant editor is capable, so Teddy just oversees and troubleshoots. I've heard that working together can be hard on a marriage, but so far, it's worked well for the two of us.

My relationship with my mother-in-law has changed for the better. My intuition served me well that day when I reassured her that I would never take her son away. We now teasingly call each other Mrs. Damsky Senior and Mrs. Damsky Junior.

"Let's go for a walk Hannah," Teddy says, as I get up to join him. I wonder what this is about.

As we stroll, hand in hand, Teddy relates a conversation he had with Uncle Ben. Teddy still goes to the office regularly for his back treatments, so he sees my dear uncle even more than I do.

"I have been asking about Tessie each week. Your uncle is reluctant to discuss the case with me. But he knows of our close relationship with Tessie. This week he revealed some information, Hannah. He asked me to share it with you. After all, we're all family now.

Dr. Ben said the radiation isn't helping Tessie anymore. She gave it a good try. But the tumor is growing. Tests and X-rays don't lie. She's had a fall and a stroke which has left her with some permanent weaknesses."

I am silent. Even shocked. Maybe I knew it in my heart, but to hear the words? I know that Tessie has a strong will to survive. She wanted to be alive to see and hold her new grandchild, and for Alvin's Bar Mitzvah. Yes, she lived for those joyful events. But maybe her luck has run out."

Teddy has the sense to let me absorb this news. He slows his pace. "Let's sit down on the bench over there," he points. As we sit down, he holds me close. We stay that way for a long time, in silence. The more I try to be strong, the more my eyes well up with tears. Teddy takes a handkerchief from his pocket and hands it to me, which brings on more tears.

"Just let it out, Hannah," Teddy says. And I do.

# An Oval Frame

Alice greets me at the door of 1235 Bloomfield Street. They have just taken Tessie home from the hospital. Alice prepares me, "Mother is not the same. They say she had a stroke. Her speech is slurred, and she broke her arm when she fell. Her face has fallen on one side. Her mouth is drooping a bit."

I grab Alice and hug her tight. She collapses in my arms. "I'm so sorry darling," I say. "To see your strong mother this way is more than we both can bear."

Alice knows how close we are, Tessie and I. I'm afraid to walk in and see her. But I know I must. Hand in hand, Alice and I approach the bedroom.

"How is my dearest friend in the world?" I say, trying to sound confident and cheerful. Tessie tries to answer me, but her words are so garbled that I can't understand her. Seeing her like this is one of the hardest things I've ever experienced.

"Let me do the talking today, Tessie," I say.

I proceed to tell her about the radio show and the people I've been meeting while working at the station. I talk about

269

the speaking engagements and I try some funny little anecdotes. I'm probably talking too much because soon, Tessie's eyes close, and her breathing becomes regular. Sleep takes over, sweet slumber. I gently give Tessie a kiss on the cheek and Alice and I tiptoe out of the room.

Alvin is standing outside the door, holding a deck of cards, a quarter, and a magic wand. He fumbles with them and says, "I've been practicing some magic tricks to show Mother. I want to cheer her up. She's going to get better right, Mrs. Damsky? She's not going to die."

And now the advice giver is completely and utterly stumped. To give the child false hope would be cruel. And to be honest feels even more cruel. I reach down and give Alvin a big hug, and say, "We will do everything in our power to keep her with us, my wonderful Bar Mitzvah boy, or should I say man? After all, the rabbi said you are a man now Alvin, right?" With that Alvin laughs and goes outside to play stickball.

As I walk downstairs I find Simon in his workshop. He's working on a large oval frame. "This was in the neighbor's trash pile. Look at it, Hannah, a perfectly good frame, gold leaf even. Who would throw this away? So maybe it's a little broken. I can fix it, and repaint it, gold leaf. When I'm done it will look just like new. I have a plan for it, "he tells me proudly.

"And what is your plan Simon, you fixer-of-all-things?" I tease him. "I bet you're going to keep me in suspense."

"That's right Hannah. My little secret." He goes back to work. Simon is a man of few words. But those big hands are always doing something important.

"How is your cleaning business going Simon?" I ask.

"We have two more customers, Hannah. Richard has been a big help, and Joe too. I'm still mad at that *mamzer*, but I guess I have to forgive him. After all, look at my little Ruthie.

Alice has been going door-to-door on Washington Street to get us new customers. She brings Ruthie with her in the carriage. My Alice is so beautiful and Ruthie so cute, who could say no?"

"I see what you mean. And I know you do good work Simon. You deserve your success. I'm glad you are treating Joe a little better now. After all, he's your son-in-law."

Simon looks up from his work, eyes looking directly into mine. "We will need to stick together now that Tessie is so weak." He looks down again and continues to work on the frame. Simon knows.

After saying goodbye I can't wait to get home to my own life. If I stay too long, I might fall apart. I want to stay strong for the Lesters. I hope to be there for them when they need me.

The next day I walk over to Uncle Ben's office. "I need to know, dear Uncle. Please help me to understand. I want to know, but I don't want to know, crazy as that sounds."

"Hannah, your friend was actually quite lucky, in that she lived longer than most people with her diagnosis. I firmly believe that her strong will to live has kept her alive up until now. Would you say that Tessie believes in God?"

I think for a moment. "Well, Simon was never very religious, so it was difficult for Tessie to be observant. Simon proudly considered himself a *free thinker, a socialist.* They both want to be *real Americans.* But I think Tessie is quietly spiritual. They don't go to synagogue much, only on the high holidays. She must have strong belief and faith in her very own private way. But Tessie is part of the Sisterhood and a member of *Pioneer Women.* I'm telling you this Uncle Ben, because the Lesters may need their faith now. It will help them to cope. Especially Simon. Uncle Ben, how much time does Tessie have? Please be honest with me."

Uncle Ben gently answers, "I can't tell you for sure, Hannah, but not much longer now. The tumor has grown substantially. It will be merciful if she doesn't suffer for too long."

# A Final Goodbye

Tessie lived one week more. During that week, Cousin Richard finished his portrait of our beloved Tessie. He used an old photo so that she looked like she did before the disease ravaged her face and body. He and Simon had it all planned. Simon's refinished, gilded oval frame was perfect for the portrait. There she is, black hair in curls, navy blue dress, and a cameo around her neck and a knowing smile on her face with a sideways glance. It's hanging over the mantle in the parlor. She was able to see it the day before she died. It's in a place of honor, right where Tessie belongs.

My dear friend died in her sleep. Uncle Ben said she probably had another stroke, this one fatal. The local burial society took care of her final needs. The ladies of the sisterhood helped the family with the *shiva* ritual. The children were devastated, especially Alvin. To hear Simon say *The Mourner's Kaddish* made me weep. He recited the Hebrew words with great emotion and quiet strength. He rose to the occasion.

*"Yis gaddal vey yisgaddash shmay rabbaw…….*

The week was a time of sadness for us all, but in some strange way it was a relief. Tessie's suffering is over now.

Mirrors were covered as guests were welcomed to pay their respects. We tried to keep Alvin busy taking care of Ruthie. I worry about him the most. He worshipped his mother. They had a special kind of bond. Perhaps because Simon was so hard on Alvin, Tessie made up for it in her own fierce, protective way.

Alice, Joe and Ruthie will move into 1235 Bloomfield St. next week, with Simon's blessing. He knows he can't take care of the boarding house and Alvin by himself. During the *shiva* week, Joe and Simon embraced, and Simon broke down and wept in Joe's arms. All of their anger fell away. It was shocking and also a relief to see this hulk of a man so vulnerable.

Irene helped out during the shiva, serving coffee and pastries. Richard was always by her side. My double batch of mandel bread was all gone by the first day. Teddy's sisters came, and his mother arrived with them, proudly carrying her sponge cake. She's made some progress, leaving her home for a special occasion like this. I was so pleased that she came. I let her know how much that meant to me.

And now, the shiva week is over. Back in Washington Heights, I sit in my new spacious apartment. I'm at the kitchen table, holding one of my fancy new china teacups, eating one last piece of mandel bread. Solly and Teddy are in the parlor listening to their radio program. And I'm alone with my thoughts.

Would Abe ever have believed my life now? And the kids' lives? We never could have predicted this back in the early years of our marriage. Do I miss Abe? Of course. But God has sent me Teddy. Life is even sweeter now.

But the passing of my dear friend has left a big hole in my life. What will I do when I have exciting news, or stories of my mother-in-law, or problems with my children? To whom will I confess my deepest fears? Where will I get that whiff of *Evening in Paris*? Who will make me laugh when things get sad?

I'm weary. I walk into the bedroom to lie down, and find an envelope on my pillow. I look at it suspiciously and open it.

*Barbara Pressman*

# Help Me Hannah # 18

*I have written to you before. You have always given me good advice. I need your counsel once again.*

*I have a wife that I love very much. We have been happy together.*

*Now she has suffered a tremendous loss. Can you give me some advice on how to help her ease the pain?*

*A Helpless Husband*

As a tear rolls down my cheek, I write:

*Dear Helpless Husband,*

*You don't even know how powerful you are.*

*Because of you, I've accomplished more in my life than I ever could have imagined, thanks to your love and encouragement.*

*Yes, I've lost a dear friend. And that friendship kept me grounded for so many years, the years when I needed a friend the most. I was lucky to have Tessie Lester in my life.*

*You ask, "How can I ease the pain?" The same way you always do. Just by being you. That's all. Stay by my side, through good times and bad …*

I continue to write, but then I drop my pen. Teddy is standing next to the bed. I stand up as he holds me close.

He kisses me gently and then with passion. My sadness washes away in the warmth of his loving arms.

"Yes, Teddy, just like that. Just like you always do."

# Epilogue

Despite hardship and pain, life goes on. Even death can be a blessing when someone is suffering. So was the case of Tessie.

She remained the centerpiece of life on 1235 Bloomfield Street. After all, you couldn't ignore that portrait above the mantle in the parlor. She looks like *The Hoboken Mona Lisa*, haunting smile and all.

Alice kept the family together. The boarding house stayed occupied with sailors from the docks. The cleaning business became even more successful now that Joe and Simon had resumed speaking to one another.

Alvin and Ruthie became very close, Alvin was Ruthie's protector. She would sit for hours watching Alvin's magic tricks. She thought he was the greatest, even better than Harry Houdini. Alvin went on to become a dentist. He performed magic tricks for the kids in his office. He continued to write wonderful poetry throughout his life.

Richard and Irene quietly married at City Hall. Although their respective families were not too happy, they didn't care. They were in love and that was that. They lived a few blocks away from the Lesters on Washington Street. They respected one another's religions. Richard attended Midnight Mass with Irene, and Irene would go to shul with

Richard on the High Holidays. Richard once confided in Hannah that he felt safer being married to a Christian woman because of the persecution he lived through in Europe. Richard painted a beautiful mural in the famous Hoboken eatery, *The Clam Broth House.* People loved it. He went on to paint many more.

Teddy finally became a "father". One day Solly said, "Would it be alright if I called you Dad?" From that day on they were truly father and son.

Solly tried out for the lead in his high school play, *The Pirates of Penzance,* and of course, he got the part. Acting remained his passion. He became a fine salesman, and enjoyed acting on the side, but as a hobby only.

Franny's letters came weekly. She was a woman with a purpose, living in Israel her whole life. The family would send her food, clothing. and, of course, the little blue JNF boxes. Hannah, Teddy, and Solly visited Franny many times throughout the years. They were thrilled when Israel became a state in 1948. You could hear the cheering all the way from Washington Heights to New Jersey.

As for Hannah, she worked hard trying to keep up with all the *Help Me Hannah* letters. The volume grew weekly. Eventually she needed a full-time staff. Teddy stayed on as her business manager. She was offered a column in a few major newspapers, and chose to write for one. Later, she became syndicated. Being a celebrity was more than Hannah ever dreamed of.

There is one thing this author knows for certain. There will always be a need for advice. The sharing of life's problems is what makes us human. So, here's to all the advice givers; Dr. Ruth, Dr. Laura, Dear Abby, Ann Landers, but especially to my inspiration, *Help Me Hannah*.

# Glossary of Yiddish Expressions

*Balabuster* – talented homemaker
*Beshert* – meant to be
*Bintel Brief* – a bundle of letters
*Bonditt* – bandit
*Bubbie* – grandmother
*Bris* – ritual circumcision
*Chutzpah* – courage, guts
*Flanken* – soup meat
*Halutzim* - Pioneers
*Gelt* – *money, gold*
*Goldena Medina* – Golden land (streets are paved with gold)
*Gonnif* – thief
*Greener* – greenhorn, new immigrant
*Kaddish* – prayer for the dead
*Kinder* - Children
*Kinehora* – an expression to ward off the evil eye
*Landsmen* – countrymen, people who are from your village or city in
　　　　　Europe
*L'Chaim* – to good health
*Macher* – big shot
*Mamzer* - bastard
*Mandel* – almonds
*Mazel Tov* – congratulations or good luck
*Mein* – my
*Mein zissen boychik* – my sweet little boy
*Mensch* – a man of fine character
*Meshugenah*– crazy
*Mishbuchah* – family
*Mitzvah* – a good deed
*Nosh* – a little bite to eat
*Nu* – "what's new?" or "go on"
*Oy gevalt* – expression of surprise, shock, or "woe is me"
*Qvell* – to be proud of
*Shayna maydele* – pretty girl
*Shiva* – period of mourning after burial, traditionally one week
*Shonda* – embarrassment, shame
*Shul* – synagogue
*Tzedukah* – charity
*Tzimmes* – both a tasty dish to eat, or a big mess, a big "to do"

283

*Yiddishe Kup* - a Jewish head
*Zay Gezunt* – to your good health, usually used when departing